Half and Half

WRITTEN BY

SOWMYASHREE S TALAWAR

About the author

Sowmyashree S Talawar is a passionate writer who found her love for storytelling after finishing her studies. She enjoys writing about a variety of themes, often drawing inspiration from everyday life and the emotions people experience. Her first novel takes readers on a heartfelt journey with characters they can connect with. When she's not writing, Sowmyashree loves to relax with a good book..

Instagram @sowmyashree_talawar

Half and Half
© 2025 Sowmyashree S Talawar
All rights reserved.

This is a work of fiction. Names, characters, places, and incidents are either the product of the author's imagination or used fictitiously. Any resemblance to actual persons, living or dead, events, or locales is entirely coincidental.

Published by Sowmyashree S Talawar
Cover Design by Ankith Kuinthodu

First Edition – 2025

For rights inquiries, contact:
sowmyashreetalawar@gmail.com

This book is dedicated to my siblings my younger and eldest one the one who listen to my blabbing all the time and one who is proud of me even when I'm doing nothing

Chapter 1

Sitar

Moving isn't hard. Leaving is.

I stared at the half-packed boxes in my apartment, clothes spilling out like they were trying to escape too. Scripts, photographs, and pieces of a life I wasn't sure I wanted anymore. The walls felt closer today, suffocating me with memories I'd rather forget.
I thought this place would feel like home eventually. It never did.

Maybe the new apartment will be better. Maybe it won't.

It didn't matter. It was closer to the shoot location, and that was reason enough.

I shoved the last box closed, grabbed my bag, and slammed the door behind me without looking back.

The new apartment building stood like any other—cracked walls, peeling paint, and the faint smell of damp concrete lingering in the hallways. Chintu, the landlord, was waiting for me downstairs. His shirt was wrinkled, his smile too polite, like he was hiding something.

"Apartment 222," he mumbled, handing me the key. His fingers lingered for a second too long.

I frowned. "Is there a problem?"

He shook his head quickly. "No, no problem. Just… welcome."

I didn't believe him, but I wasn't here to make friends or investigate his weirdness. I was here to forget everything else.

I climbed the stairs, the old metal railing cold beneath my fingers. When I reached the door, I slid the key in. But before I could turn it, the door creaked open.

Unlocked?

My heart skipped. Maybe Chintu forgot to lock it after the last showing. Or maybe—

Don't overthink. Just check.
I pushed the door open cautiously.

And froze.

People. In my apartment.

They moved around like they belonged—arranging furniture, unpacking boxes, laughing like this was their home.
I stood there, stunned, my grip tightening around the keys until they dug into my palm.

"What the—"

Before I could finish, a man stepped out of one of the rooms, holding a file. He was tall, with sharp features and a gaze that sliced right through me. His suit was too crisp for someone moving in, his expression too calm for someone caught trespassing.

Our eyes met. The air felt heavier.

"Who are you?" I snapped; my voice louder than I intended.

He raised an eyebrow, his face tightening with annoyance. "I should be asking you the same. This is my apartment."

"Your apartment?" My voice shot up an octave. "This is my apartment!"
We both launched into shouting, voices overlapping in a chaotic mess of accusations.

"I signed the lease last week!"
"I signed it a month ago!"
"Chintu!" I bellowed, storming toward the door.

But before I could call him again, something strange happened.

A gust of wind swept through the room, sharp and cold. The windows were shut. The door barely open.

The lights flickered.

We both froze.

"Did you feel that?" he asked, his voice quieter now, tinged with something unfamiliar fear.

I nodded slowly, my eyes scanning the room. "What was that?"

Then we heard it.

A soft, haunting melody. The delicate strings of a sitar, plucked gently, almost as if the notes themselves were floating in the air.

The sound seemed to come from nowhere. And everywhere.

Our eyes met—not with hostility this time, but with confusion.

"Chintu?" I whispered again.
No response.

Chapter 2
Aniket

This was not part of the plan.

I didn't like surprises. I liked schedules, contracts, things that made sense. But there I was, standing in what was supposed to be my apartment, arguing with a woman who had a voice sharp enough to cut glass and an attitude to match.

Her name was Sitara—I'd caught it when she yelled at the landlord over the phone. She was an actress, apparently, based on the scripts scattered around her boxes. The kind of person who thrived on drama, both on-screen and off.

Chintu arrived finally, sweating and breathless like he'd run from the first floor—which he probably had.

"What is going on?" he asked, looking between us.

"Oh, you tell us," Sitara snapped. "Why are there two people with keys to the same apartment?"

Chintu's face went pale. "I—uh—it wasn't intentional. There was a mix-up with the paperwork. Our new assistant… made a mistake."

I crossed my arms. "Fix it."

Sitara mirrored me, her glare sharp enough to set him on fire. "Yeah. Fix it."
Chintu's nervous laugh filled the silence. "Well, technically… you both signed valid leases. So, um… maybe you could—"

"If you're about to suggest we live together, I swear—" I started.

"—Why can't you both live here?" he blurted out anyway, his words tumbling out in desperation. "It's a three-bedroom apartment. You can split the rent. Separate rooms. Shared space. Easy solution!"
I stared at him like he'd grown a second head.
"Live with her?" I scoffed. "No way."

"With him?" Sitara echoed, just as horrified. "Absolutely not."

Chintu held up his hands. "Look, it's either that, or you both leave, and I'll have to refund the deposits—which I, uh… don't have right now."

The thought of starting apartment hunting again made my stomach twist. Sitara looked equally annoyed, chewing on her bottom lip like she was fighting the same battle in her head.

After a long, tense silence, she sighed. "Fine. But only until I find another place."
I clenched my jaw. "Agreed. This is temporary."

Chintu practically collapsed with relief. "Great! I'll finalize the paperwork."

As he left, Sitara and I exchanged a glance—not friendly, not hostile. Just… resigned.
This was going to be a nightmare.

Chapter 3
Rules

Before signing the legal agreement, Aniket cleared his throat, stepping forward with his usual commanding presence. "If we're going to live under the same roof, we need to establish some ground rules. I have a few conditions."

Sitara, leaning against the wall with her arms crossed, raised an eyebrow. "Oh, this should be good. Let's hear it, Mr. Lawyer."

Aniket ignored her sarcasm and began listing his rules, his tone firm and precise:
1. "No loud noises after 9 PM. I have important meetings and need my rest."
2. "The kitchen will be cleaned immediately after use. No dishes left in the sink."
3. "Absolutely no unauthorized guests. This is a private space."
4. "Shared spaces like the living room must remain clutter-free at all times."
5. "We will divide the grocery shopping equally and stick to a written list."
6. "The third room is off-limits to you. I'll use it as my study."

Sitara blinked at him, her lips twitching as if trying not to laugh. "Wow. Are we roommates or coworkers? You're running this place like a law firm."

"I believe in structure," Aniket replied, adjusting his tie. "Now, if you're done mocking me, do you have any rules?"

Sitara straightened up, a mischievous glint in her eyes. "Oh, I have rules. You're not the only one with standards, Mr. CEO." She started listing her own, her tone overly dramatic:

1. "No suits in the living room. This is a casual zone. Leave your corporate vibes at the door."
2. "The TV remote is mine during my serial timings. No exceptions."
3. "You can't complain if I practice my lines out loud. My acting comes first."
4. "If you're going to eat snacks, you better share. I don't care if it's your diet granola bar."
5. "The third room is off-limits to you. I'll use it for rehearsals."

Aniket stared at her, incredulous. "You can't just copy my rule about the third room!"
"Why not? You don't own exclusivity over rules," she shot back with a grin.

Chintu, who had been quietly observing, looked like he was about to burst into laughter but wisely kept his mouth shut.

"Fine," Aniket said through gritted teeth. "But let's be clear—this is a temporary arrangement. I don't plan on entertaining your... eccentricities for long."

"Likewise," Sitara said, her smile fading slightly as she glanced at the legal agreement. "Let's just get this over with."

They both signed the document, their signatures bold and deliberate, as if marking the start of a battle.

As Chintu handed them the keys, he muttered, "Good luck. You'll need it."

Chapter 4
The First Day of Rules

The morning started innocently enough—deceptively peaceful, like the calm before a storm.

Aniket emerged from his room at precisely 7:00 AM, dressed impeccably in a crisp white shirt, his tie perfectly aligned, and his laptop bag slung over his shoulder. His hair was as neat as his life—or at least how he liked to pretend it was.

Meanwhile, I was sprawled on the couch in my "I'm-off-duty" pajamas, munching on a bag of chips, crumbs decorating the blanket like little confetti. The TV blared my favourite serial, the dramatic background score filling the room.

Aniket cleared his throat, clearly annoyed. "Rule four: Shared spaces must remain clutter-free," he said, glancing pointedly at the mess of chip packets and soda cans around me.

I didn't even bother looking at him. "Rule one: No suits in the living room. This is a casual zone," I shot back, lazily popping another chip into my mouth.

His jaw clenched as he sighed dramatically, slipping off his blazer and draping it neatly over a chair. "Happy?"
I smirked. "Ecstatic."

And that's how it began—a battle of unspoken one-upmanship.

Scene 1: The Third Room Standoff

At 11:00 AM, Aniket marched toward the third room with a stack of legal documents, his expression screaming "I'm busy and important."

But when he opened the door, there I was—standing in the middle of the room, dramatically rehearsing a monologue, my scripts scattered across the floor like confetti.

"What are you doing in here?" he demanded, his voice dripping with disbelief.

"Rehearsing," I replied casually, flipping a page. "Rule five: This room is for my rehearsals."

His eyes narrowed. "Rule six: This room is my study."

We stood there, glaring at each other in complete silence.

Then I smirked. "Rock-paper-scissors for it?"

He blinked. "No."

"Scared you'll lose?"

Without another word, he spun on his heel and stormed out, muttering something about "childish behaviour."

Victory: Sitara - 1 | Aniket - 0

Scene 2: The TV Remote War

By 7:00 PM, I had claimed my throne—couch, blanket, snacks, and the most powerful weapon of all: the TV remote.

Aniket walked in, glancing at his watch as if it could somehow justify him interrupting my sacred serial time.

"I have an important webinar," he announced, holding up his laptop like it was a trophy.

"Cool," I said, not taking my eyes off the screen. "Rule two: The TV remote is mine during my serial timings. No exceptions."

"You can't just—" he started, but I cut him off.

"Headphones," I said sweetly, pointing at the pair lying on the coffee table.

His eye twitched, but he plugged in his headphones, glaring at me like I'd personally ruined his career.

Victory: Sitara - 2 | Aniket - 0
Scene 3: Snack Sabotage

Later that night, Aniket tried to sneak into the kitchen, quietly opening a packet of granola bars like a ninja on a secret mission.

But I appeared out of nowhere—like the snack police.

"Rule four: Share your snacks," I declared, holding out my hand.

"They're protein bars," he grumbled, clearly regretting every life choice that led him to this moment.

"Doesn't matter. A rule's a rule."

Grumbling, he handed me one. I took a bite— and immediately regretted it.

"This tastes like cardboard," I mumbled, chewing reluctantly.

"Then why did you want it?" he snapped.

"Principle," I replied with a shrug, tossing the rest into the trash.

Victory: Sitara - 3 | Aniket – 0

Scene 4: The AC Battle
Later that evening, I curled up on the couch with a blanket, shivering dramatically.
"It's freezing in here!" I complained, grabbing the AC remote.

Aniket, seated at the dining table with his laptop, glanced up. "The AC is set to 24°C. That's perfectly comfortable."

"Comfortable? For a polar bear, maybe!" I exclaimed, turning it up to 28°C.

Without missing a beat, he grabbed the remote and turned it back down.

"This is a shared space. We keep it reasonable," he said firmly.

"Reasonable? I'm turning into an icicle!" I shot back, snatching the remote again.

And so began the great AC tug-of-war—click, snatch, click, snatch—until Chintu walked in, looking at us like we were unruly kids fighting over a toy.

"What's going on now?" he asked, crossing his arms.

"She's trying to turn the living room into a sauna!" Aniket said, pointing at me like I was the villain.
"He's trying to turn it into a freezer!" I countered, crossing my arms.
Chintu sighed, walking over and snatching the remote from both of us. "You two sound like an old married couple fighting over the AC. It's embarrassing."

Aniket and I glared at him in unison. "We are NOT a couple!" we shouted together.

Chintu rolled his eyes, setting the AC to 26°C. "I'm locking this remote in my room if either of you touches it again."

As he walked away, I muttered, "You should've been a judge, not a landlord."

"And you should wear a sweater," Aniket added, earning another glare from me.

Chintu stopped at the doorway, gave us both a pitying look, and sighed dramatically. "Good luck, AC. You're going to need it."

Final score: Sitara - 3 | Aniket - 1 (with Chintu's assist)

Later That Night

The apartment finally fell silent. The faint hum of the AC was the only sound—until it wasn't.

A loud "VICTORY DANCE TIME!" echoed through the hallway, followed by the unmistakable sound of cheesy pop music blaring from the speakers.

I burst out of my room, wearing sunglasses and waving a makeshift victory flag made from an old bedsheet. My dramatic dance moves were an odd mix of enthusiasm and zero coordination, but I owned every second of it.

Aniket stepped out of his room, rubbing his temples like he had an important meeting with his sanity. "Seriously?" he groaned, his voice laced with exhaustion.

"Rule seven," I announced proudly, striking a ridiculous pose, "The winner of the day gets to celebrate however they want!"

He sighed, shaking his head, but there was the faintest trace of a smile tugging at the corner of his mouth—like he hated losing but secretly enjoyed this chaotic ritual.

As I spun around dramatically, almost tripping over the flag, I caught him chuckling under his breath.

"Admit it," I said, pointing at him with exaggerated flair. "You love this."

Aniket rolled his eyes. "I tolerate it."

But as he walked back to his room, I heard him mutter softly, just loud enough for me to catch:
"Tolerate it way more than I should."

Final score: Sitara - 4 | Aniket - 1 (and secretly loving it)

Chapter 5
Quiet day

The morning after the chaotic rule day was eerily… calm. The apartment, usually alive with Sitara's sarcastic quips and Aniket's exasperated sighs, felt strangely hollow.

Aniket noticed the difference immediately. No snarky comments when he walked into the kitchen. No loud declarations of victory. No Sitara dramatically proclaiming herself the "Queen of the Apartment" like she'd won some prestigious award for surviving another day of their petty battles.

Instead, Sitara was sitting quietly at the dining table, sipping her coffee—black, no sugar, no fuss. She wasn't even slouched lazily like usual. Her posture was straight, almost too proper, as if she was trying to hold herself together with invisible threads.

Aniket frowned. Something was definitely off.

By afternoon, the silence grew unbearable. It wasn't the peaceful kind of silence he'd always claimed to crave. This was the uncomfortable, heavy kind—the kind that felt like it had weight.

Unable to concentrate on his work, he finally closed his laptop with a frustrated sigh and wandered into the living room, leaning against the doorframe like he owned the place.

"You're... behaving strangely," he blurted out.

Sitara, cross-legged on the couch, scrolling aimlessly through her phone, didn't even glance up. "Strangely how?"

"You're being... polite. Considerate. It's unsettling." His eyes narrowed slightly, scanning her face for any clue.

She sighed, locking her phone and setting it aside. "I have an award function tomorrow. I don't have time to bother you. Happy?"

Aniket raised an eyebrow. "That's not it." He stepped further into the room, plopping onto the armchair across from her. "What's really going on?"

There was a brief pause. Sitara picked at a loose thread on the cushion, her fingers fidgeting in a way that betrayed her calm façade. Then she muttered quietly, "It's the first award function I'm attending since... since my mom passed away."

Her voice faltered on the last part, barely above a whisper. She quickly looked away, blinking hard like she could the sting behind her eyes to disappear.

Aniket's heart did this weird thing—like a stumble. He wasn't good at this emotional stuff. His life was built around logic, rules, facts. Emotions didn't fit neatly into that framework. But seeing Sitara, usually so bold and unapologetically loud, look this small? That hit differently.

"Oh," he said dumbly, because what else was there to say?

She gave a tight, hollow smile. "There's no one to come with me. It's supposed to be a big night, but… it doesn't feel like it."

Aniket shifted uncomfortably, glancing at the floor like it might provide the right words. "I'm not exactly the kind of person you'd want to take to something like that. You should ask Chintu."

"He's busy," she replied quickly. "And I don't have anyone else."

Her voice wasn't bitter or self-pitying. It was just… matter of fact. That's what made it worse.

Aniket frowned. "Why not? You're funny, outgoing— making friends should be easy for you."

Sitara let out a soft, dry laugh. "Yeah, well. There's something… I don't know. Some kind of curse, maybe. I've never had close friends. People just don't stick around."

The words hung between them, heavier than the silence that followed.

"That's ridiculous," he said after a moment, his tone softer than usual. "You're funny, yes. Annoying, definitely. But you're also… not terrible to be around. Most of the time."

Sitara snorted despite herself. "Wow. What a glowing review. 'Not terrible to be around.' I should get that on a T-shirt."

Aniket smirked slightly, leaning back in the chair. "Could be your new brand."

For a moment, the tension eased, replaced by something warmer.

Then, without really thinking, Aniket added, "Look, if it means that much to you… I'll go."
Sitara's head snapped up. "Wait. What?"
"I'll go with you. But only because I can't stand watching you mope around. It's… annoying."

Her eyes widened, processing his words like they were in a foreign language. "You'd come with me?"

"Don't read too much into it," he said quickly, his ears turning slightly pink. "I just don't want you ruining the apartment with your 'sad energy.'"
She stared at him for a long moment, then—slowly—a genuine smile crept onto her face. Not her usual smug grin, but something softer. Something real.

"Thanks, Mr. Lawyer," she whispered. "I'll try not to embarrass you too much."

He rolled his eyes, but the corners of his mouth twitched upward. "No promises on my end."

As he stood to leave, she called after him, "Hey, Aniket?"

He turned, one hand on the doorframe.

"You're not completely useless, you know."

He chuckled softly. "Yeah, well. Don't get used to it."

But as he walked away, his smile lingered longer than usual. And for once, he didn't mind.

Chapter 6
The Award Night

The grand hall shimmered under golden lights, filled with celebrities, flashing cameras, and an eager crowd. Sitara sat in her designated seat, dressed in an elegant black saree, her hair cascading down her shoulders. She glanced at her phone—no new messages.

"Hey, are you on your way?"

"It's about to start."

"Aniket?"

No reply.

She sighed, forcing herself to focus on the event. The loud applause, the laughter, the flashing lights—it all felt distant, muted. Last year, she sat in a similar chair, waiting with her mother by her side. She hadn't won then, but her mother's reassuring smile had been enough. "You've already won in my eyes," her mother had whispered.

But this year was different. She was alone. Or at least, she thought she wouldn't be. She'd believed Aniket would be there. He promised.
As the announcer called out nominees for Best Actress, her heart raced—not with excitement, but with

disappointment, her eyes still searching the crowd for a face she knew wouldn't be there.

"And the winner is… Sitara!"

The applause thundered around her, but her heart was heavy. She walked to the stage, her steps steady even though her emotions were anything but. The bright lights felt harsher tonight. The award, though beautiful, felt colder in her hands.

As she turned to face the crowd, the LED screen behind her displayed her journey—a montage of her performances. And then, unexpectedly, the last photo she'd taken with her mother appeared.

Her mother's radiant smile filled the screen. It wasn't just a picture; it was a memory she'd been trying to avoid for six long months. The tears came fast, unstoppable, blurring the lights and faces in front of her.

She gripped the microphone, her voice caught somewhere between her chest and throat. After a long, suffocating pause, she managed to whisper, "This is for her," pointing at the screen where her mother's face beamed back at her.

She didn't wait for the applause. She walked off the stage, clutching the award like it was both a trophy and a burden.

Chapter 7
Bittu

Sitara returned to her apartment late that night, the award tucked under her arm. The silence of the empty hall felt louder than the roaring applause from earlier.

She opened the door, expecting nothing—just the usual emptiness. But there was Aniket, sitting on the couch, looking dishevelled, his tie loose, frustration evident on his face.

Before she could say anything, he stood up, holding something behind his back. "I know I messed up," he blurted, his words tumbling over each other. "I wanted to be there. I swear, Sitara. I got stuck with work, and it wasn't supposed to—"
She walked past him, placing the award silently on the table.

"I'm sorry," he whispered, guilt etched into his face.

She didn't respond. Instead, she sat down, her eyes distant, her fingers grazing the edge of the cold trophy.

Aniket sighed, then revealed what he'd been hiding—a small fishbowl, with a tiny, vibrant fish swimming inside. The water sparkled under the dim lights, and the fish's colourful fins flickered like flames.

"Meet Bittu," he said awkwardly, trying to lighten the tension. "I figured… if I couldn't be there for you tonight, maybe he could."
Sitara blinked at the little creature, its tiny body darting around in the bowl. Despite herself, she let out a soft, shaky laugh.

"A fish?" she muttered, wiping at her eyes.

"Yeah. Low maintenance, no drama… and it won't talk back," he said with a small smile, echoing his words from the day he'd brought her a fish before.

Sitara glanced at Bittu, then at Aniket. The anger she'd carried all evening began to dissolve—not because of the fish, but because of him.

She reached out, tapping the glass gently, watching the fish swim closer. "He's cute," she whispered.

Aniket sat beside her, his shoulder barely brushing against hers. "You're not alone, Sitara. You never were."

She didn't respond with words. Instead, she leaned her head on his shoulder, closing her eyes, feeling the warmth she'd been craving—not from the applause, not from the award, but from someone who cared.
And maybe, just maybe, that was enough.

Chapter 8
Fear of loving

The next morning, sunlight streamed through the thin curtains of Sitara's apartment, casting golden patterns on the floor. She sat cross-legged in front of the small fishbowl, watching Bittu swim in lazy circles. Its vibrant fins fluttered like delicate silk ribbons in water.

She'd woken up feeling light, a rare sensation since her mother's passing. The memory of Aniket's awkward apology, his dishevelled look, and the fishbowl gift had made her blush under her blanket. She hadn't felt this kind of warmth in a long time.
But warmth was dangerous.

The feeling crept in slowly—a knot tightening in her chest. Her heart reminded her of an old, painful belief: everyone you love leaves you. First her father when she was just a child in 5th grade. Then Vedhant, her best friend in 12th, whose truth was too heavy for his family to bear. And then her mother—her last anchor—gone in an instant, leaving her adrift.

She stared at Bittu, her throat tightening. What if I start loving you, and you die too?

Panic rising, she grabbed the fishbowl and stormed out, her heart racing faster than her footsteps.

Aniket's door creaked open, revealing him still in his pajamas, hair tousled, holding a mug of coffee. Before he could greet her, Sitara thrust the fishbowl into his hands.

"Take it back," she blurted, her voice shaky.

Aniket blinked, confused. "What? Did he—uh—poop too much? I heard fish do that sometimes."

"This isn't funny," she snapped, her voice trembling. "Just… take him back."

Aniket sobered immediately, setting the mug down and gently placing Bittu on the table. "Tara, what's wrong?"

She hesitated, staring at her feet before whispering, "Everyone I love dies."

His playful smirk faded.

"My dad. Vedhant. My mom. Now this stupid fish. I don't want to care about him because… because what if he dies too?"

Aniket was silent for a moment, absorbing her words. Then, without warning, he burst out laughing.

Sitara scowled. "Are you serious right now?"
He wiped away a tear from laughing too hard. "Tara, if that's the case, I have the perfect solution."
She glared at him. "What?"

"Fall in love with me," he declared dramatically, placing a hand over his heart like a Shakespearean actor. "That way, I'll die, and problem solved!"

Sitara stared at him, her jaw dropping. "Shiii! Love? With you? Are you out of your mind?"

Aniket gasped, mock offended. "Wow. You didn't even hesitate. That was faster than rejecting spam calls."

Despite herself, she laughed—a real, belly-deep laugh that she hadn't felt in ages. The sound echoed around the room, chasing away the heaviness.

He grinned, satisfied. "See? That's the point. If laughter can survive, so can love. People don't die because you love them, Tara. They just… die. It's life. But you? You're still here. You're the constant."

She stared at him, her heart softening. He always knew how to pull her back from the edge, even if it meant making a fool of himself.

Aniket picked up Bittu, holding the bowl like a trophy. "This little guy isn't going anywhere. He's a survivor. And so are you."
Sitara rolled her eyes, snatching the fishbowl back. "Fine. But if he dies, you're responsible."

"Deal," he said with a wink.

As she walked back to her room, cradling Bittu, she realized something fascinating—maybe it wasn't the fear of losing people that haunted her. Maybe it was the fear of living without them.

And maybe, just maybe, Aniket was teaching her how to live again.

Chapter 9
Tara

Sitara didn't realize it at first—not until she was back in her room, the door closed, and the silence pressing around her like a soft blanket.

Tara.

Aniket had called her Tara.

Not once. Not twice. He'd said it like it was the most natural thing in the world. But for Sitara, that name wasn't just a nickname. It was a piece of her heart, tucked away in the corners of memories she rarely dared to visit.

Tara.

Her mother used to call her that. Tara—meaning star. "You're my star, lighting up my world," her mother would whisper, tucking her into bed with a kiss on the forehead. No one else had ever called her that. Not friends. Not teachers. Not even Vedhant.

And now… Aniket.

Without thinking, she shot up from her bed, her feet moving faster than her thoughts. She stormed into Aniket's room, her heart pounding, not even bothering to knock.

Aniket, standing there with just a towel wrapped around his waist, froze mid-step, holding a fresh T-shirt. His hair was damp, droplets of water trailing down his neck.

"You really need to stop doing that," he groaned, his eyes wide. "This is a guy's room. You've already claimed the entire apartment. Leave this space alone, at least!"

Sitara ignored his dramatic protest, her eyes burning with curiosity. "Take a break, Anni. Why did you call me that?"

He blinked. "Call you what?"

She crossed her arms, determined. "Tara. Why did you call me Tara?"

Aniket rubbed the back of his neck, clearly confused. "I… I don't know. I just felt like it."

"Felt like it?" she repeated, narrowing her eyes. "It's not just a random name. Only my mom used to call me that. It means star."

Aniket shrugged, a small grin tugging at the corner of his lips. "Maybe because you're shining like one?"
She rolled her eyes, unamused. "No cheesy lines. Just answer."

"Well," he said, thinking aloud, "maybe because everyone calls me Anni—my adopted mom used to call me that, Anni, my honey—and everyone calls you Sita. But Tara felt different. Like… it's just for you."

Sitara's heart skipped a beat. She didn't know how to respond to that.

"Why? Did your ex call you Tara?" he teased, raising an eyebrow.

She shot him a sharp glare. "No. I don't have an ex. My mom wouldn't have let me."

Aniket smirked, not missing a beat. "Well, you can have one now."
Her glare deepened, and he immediately mouthed, "Sorry!" with exaggerated puppy eyes.

She huffed, turning toward the door. "Call me Sitara. Or Sita. But not Tara."

But just as her hand touched the doorknob, his voice floated softly from behind.

"Tara."

She paused, her back still to him. A small, involuntary smile crept onto her face; one she couldn't fight. She didn't turn around. She didn't need to.
Without a word, she walked out, her heart strangely lighter.

And Aniket, standing there in nothing but a towel, smiled too—because he knew she didn't really mind.

Chapter 10
Kitchen

The morning sun filtered through the blinds, casting golden stripes across the kitchen floor. Aniket walked in at precisely 8:00 AM, his routine as rigid as ever, mentally prepared for his usual bowl of perfectly measured oatmeal with exactly seven almonds. Life was predictable, neat, and controlled—just how he liked it.

Until he saw her.

Sitara stood in the middle of the kitchen like a tornado had spun her into existence. But unlike most mornings, today the chaos smelled amazing. A large pot of steaming biryani sat on the counter, the aroma of saffron, caramelized onions, and slow-cooked spices filling the air.

Aniket blinked, his brain buffering like a slow internet connection.

"You... cooked?" he asked, his voice laced with genuine surprise.

Sitara turned around, a smug grin on her face. "As a thank-you for Bittu's gift."

Aniket hesitated. His diet dictated strict portions, calculated calories, and an aversion to anything remotely indulgent. But the fragrance of the biryani was working against him.

"I wasn't sure if you'd eat it," Sitara admitted, wiping her hands on a kitchen towel. "So, I thought I'd make something you can eat."

Aniket followed her gaze to the other side of the counter. A tray of what could generously be called "cookies" sat abandoned, burnt beyond recognition. The kitchen, which had been serene just moments ago, now resembled a battlefield—flour in her hair, batter streaked across the counter, and an unmistakable trail of destruction leading to the sink.

Aniket's eye twitched. So close. She was so close to perfection.

"What... happened here?" he croaked, unable to look away from the disaster zone.

"Cooking experiment," Sitara replied cheerfully, licking a spoon with stubborn pride. "Biryani felt too risky, so I thought I'd make cookies for breakfast. It's creative, right?"

Aniket sighed, running a hand down his face. "Cookies aren't breakfast." His cleaning instincts kicked in, and he reached for a sponge. "And rule number two: clean the kitchen immediately after use."

Sitara raised an eyebrow, unfazed. "I was going to clean it after breakfast," she said with an exaggerated shrug.

"They're burnt, Sitara!"

"They're rustic," she shot back, grinning as she picked up a charred cookie with the confidence of someone presenting fine art.

Aniket groaned, scrubbing the counter like it had personally offended him. "You're impossible! You can't just leave a mess for someone else to clean!"

"Who said I was leaving it for you? I was going to clean it after breakfast!" she snapped, her voice rising to match his.
"Oh, so this is your idea of breakfast. Burnt cookies and kitchen chaos?" He tossed the sponge into the sink with a dramatic splash.

Sitara's temper flared. "You're such a control freak, Anni! Not everything has to be done your way!"

"I'm not a control freak! I just happen to like living in a house that doesn't look like a tornado hit it!"

Without thinking, Sitara grabbed a cookie and chucked it at him.
"Here! Have a cookie! Maybe it'll sweeten your sour mood!"
Aniket dodged it with surprising agility. The cookie hit the floor with a dramatic thud, crumbling into sad, burnt fragments.

"You're insane!" he shouted, his face turning red with frustration.

Before the argument could escalate further, the door burst open. Chintu, the landlord, stumbled in, panting as if he'd run a marathon. He held his phone like a reporter chasing the next big story.

"What's going on here? The other tenants are calling, saying there's shouting and banging coming from your flat!" Chintu's eyes darted between Sitara's flour-covered face and Aniket's frazzled expression.
Aniket pointed dramatically at Sitara. "Ask her! She's the one who turned the kitchen into a war zone!"

Sitara crossed her arms, glaring at both. "I was just trying to make cookies, and someone decided to turn it into a lecture on cleanliness!"

Chintu sniffed the air and gagged slightly. "Cookies? Smells like a burnt offering to the kitchen gods."

Sitara groaned, grabbed a blanket from the couch, and wrapped herself in it like a dramatic burrito. She collapsed onto the sofa with an exaggerated sigh.
"I'm done. You two can fight over the kitchen. I'll just starve."
Aniket pinched the bridge of his nose, his patience hanging by a thread. "Chintu, please just go before you make this worse."

But Chintu wasn't done. "Should I tell the neighbours it was a kitchen disaster… or a lovers' spat?"

"OUT!" Sitara and Aniket yelled in unison, both pointing at the door like synchronized swimmers.

Chintu laughed all the way out, leaving a trail of smugness behind him.

As the door clicked shut, Aniket sighed and turned to Sitara, who peeked out from under her blanket with an exaggerated pout.

"We need to set some ground rules," he muttered, defeated.

Sitara grinned. "Rule one: No yelling before breakfast." She grabbed a pillow and lobbed it at him.

Despite himself, Aniket chuckled. "Fine. But rule two still stands—clean up your mess."

"Deal," she said, her grin widening.

As they cleaned up the mess together, Aniket finally sat down with a plate of biryani and took a bite. The explosion of flavours—perfectly cooked rice, tender meat, and the warmth of homemade spices—made him pause.

"This is…" He swallowed and looked at her, surprised. "This is really good."

Sitara shrugged nonchalantly, but her eyes sparkled. "Told you I could cook."

Aniket set his spoon down, leaning back in his chair. "I do diet… but if someone cooks for me with their full heart, I'm ready to cheat on it."

Chintu, who had sneakily returned, grinned and plopped down at the table. "Same! Pass me a plate."

Sitara laughed, serving them both while Aniket rolled his eyes.

That evening, as the kitchen filled with warm laughter and the smell of perfectly cooked biryani, Aniket realized something.

Life had become a little less predictable… and somehow, he didn't mind at all.

Chapter 11
The Birthday He Wouldn't Accept

The evening was quiet—too quiet—until a knock on the door shattered the silence. Aniket, who had been comfortably reading on the couch, groaned. He already knew who it was.

With a sigh, he stood up and opened the door to find Saanvi standing there, wearing her signature smirk, a bag slung over her shoulder.

"Surprise!" Saanvi grinned, stepping in without waiting for an invitation.

Aniket crossed his arms. "Not surprised. Just annoyed." Saanvi ignored him, plopping onto the couch. "You know, for someone who lives in a fancy apartment, you really need to upgrade your welcome reactions. Maybe throw in a fake smile at least?"

Before Aniket could retort, Sitara entered the living room, holding a plate of freshly made laddoos. She paused when she saw Saanvi, her eyebrows raising slightly.

"Who's this?" she asked, glancing between them.

"Saanvi," Aniket muttered, rubbing his temples. "My childhood headache."

"Best friend," Saanvi corrected, flashing a playful grin at Sitara.

Before Sitara could respond, Chintu entered, stretching his arms dramatically. His eyes landed on Saanvi, and within seconds, his entire posture changed. He straightened up, ran a hand through his hair, and put on his best "charming" expression.

"Well, well," Chintu said smoothly, "Ani never mentioned he had such a stunning best friend. If I'd known, I would've dropped by more often."

Saanvi raised an eyebrow. "Oh, are you the famous Chintu? Ani told me all about you."
Chintu smirked. "All good things, I hope?"

Saanvi tilted her head. "Mostly about your tragic flirting skills."

Chintu clutched his chest dramatically. "Ouch. You wound me, madam." He leaned in slightly. "But don't worry, I specialize in winning over sceptics."

Sitara rolled her eyes. "Here we go."

Aniket sighed, already regretting opening the door. "Why are you here, Saanvi?"

Saanvi's playful grin faded slightly as she leaned back, getting comfortable. "It's today, Ani. You thought I'd forget?"

Aniket's jaw tightened. "It's just a date."

"It's your birthday," Saanvi corrected, her voice softer.

Sitara frowned, looking between them. "But didn't you say your birthday is in March?"

Saanvi answered before Aniket could. "That's his official birthday. But today is the day he was adopted."

Sitara blinked, surprised. Aniket clenched his fists. "It's not a birthday, Saanvi. It's just a date on a piece of paper."

Saanvi scoffed. "You can pretend all you want, but you can't fool me. You were reborn that day, Ani. You got a family. That's worth celebrating."

Chintu, for once, didn't interrupt. He simply watched the exchange, arms crossed.

Sitara suddenly stood up. "I made biryani today," she announced. "And I made extra."
Saanvi's eyes lit up. "Biryani? Now that's a proper celebration!"

Chintu grinned. "A girl who loves biryani. I think I'm in love."

Saanvi smirked. "Sorry, but I don't date men who flirt within five minutes of meeting me."

Chintu gasped. "Then I'll wait six minutes."

As laughter filled the room, Aniket exhaled. Maybe, just maybe, some dates were worth remembering after all.

Chapter 12
Influencer

The aroma of biryani still lingered in the apartment, a testament to Sitara's late-night culinary adventure. Aniket sat at the dining table, enjoying the last few bites, his usual diet long forgotten.

Saanvi, on the other hand, was buzzing with excitement, her camera already set up on the tripod. "Ani, you have no idea how big this is! Sitara, you're already a celebrity, but with this video—BOOM! Viral!"

Sitara raised an eyebrow. "I just made biryani. What's so special about that?"

Saanvi clutched her chest dramatically. "Just made biryani. Do you even understand the emotions behind this dish? This isn't food—it's art, its poetry, it's—"

"Calories," Aniket interrupted, taking another bite.

"Exactly! And my subscribers LOVE food vlogs. But more than that, they love drama," Saanvi said, smirking as she focused the camera on the two of them.

Chintu leaned in with a sly grin. "Speaking of love, should I stand next to Saanvi for this? You know, for the chemistry?"
Saanvi rolled her eyes. "You're relentless."

Chintu winked. "And you're breathtaking."

Sitara groaned. "Can we focus?"

The video started off innocently enough—Sitara explaining the recipe, Saanvi dramatically reacting to the aroma, and Aniket quietly eating while throwing in the occasional sarcastic comment. But the moment the video went live, chaos erupted.

Fan pages exploded with clips, analysing every glance, every smile, every stolen look Aniket gave Sitara. Comments flooded in:

"Did you see how he looked at her when she wasn't watching? That's love, people!"

"Ani acts all serious, but the moment Sitara talks, he actually smiles. Smiles! This is history."

"Forget biryani. We need a wedding announcement!"

Sitara scrolled through the comments, her mouth slightly open. "Are… are they shipping us?"

Aniket, who had been quietly reading over her shoulder, groaned. "This is exactly why I don't do social media." Meanwhile, Chintu was scrolling through his own set of comments. He smirked and nudged Saanvi. "Looks like we have a fanbase too."

Saanvi peeked at his phone. "Chintu x Saanvi = Fire Couple"

She burst out laughing. "Wow. The internet ships everyone these days."

Chintu smirked. "Well, maybe they're onto something."

Saanvi gave him a challenging look. "If you're trying to flirt, you'll need better material."
Chintu leaned back, unfazed. "Don't worry. I have plenty more where that came from."

Saanvi chuckled but didn't argue.

Saanvi, meanwhile, was grinning like a mastermind. "You guys don't get it! This is gold! People love you together. The fan pages had already connected the dots before you even realized there were dots!"

Sitara buried her face in her hands. "I just wanted to cook biryani…"

Aniket exhaled sharply. "Great. Now I'm not just 'Mr. Lawyer'—I'm 'Sitara's Mystery Man'."
Chintu snorted. "More like 'Sitara's Secret Crush'."
Aniket shot him a glare. "Chintu."

Chintu raised his hands in surrender. "Fine, fine. No more teasing. But hey, look at the bright side! You're both famous now!"

Sitara peeked through her fingers. "And that's a bright side?"

Chintu chuckled. "Oh, absolutely."

Aniket sighed. His life had been quiet, structured, predictable. And then Sitara happened. Now, thanks to one viral video, the internet had declared them a couple.

He should've been annoyed, but instead… he found himself stealing a glance at Sitara, who was still staring at the screen in disbelief.

Maybe the fan pages weren't entirely wrong.

Chapter 13
Resort

Aniket leaned back on the couch, staring at his phone. His fingers hovered over the screen as he debated whether to message her or not. It had only been a few hours since Sitara left, but the apartment already felt strangely empty.

Before he could overthink it, he typed out a message:

"Where are you, Tara?"

The reply came almost instantly.

"Don't call me Tara."
Aniket smirked. Some things never changed.

"Answer my question, Tara."

"Just in case you've done anything illegal, as your roommate and a lawyer, I should be prepared to answer the police. So, tell me—where are you?"

There was a brief pause before her next message popped up.

"I'm at the resort."
His eyebrows furrowed.

"Where…?"

"Resort, you silly."

Aniket rolled his eyes.

"If you had just said so, I would've given you company."

"Ani, I'm not here to enjoy. I'm here to check the finances."

His interest piqued.

"Oh? Is it yours?"

"Of course not. It's my dad's."

That caught him off guard. He had never really asked about her family's business before.
"Can I know the name of the resort?"

The next message made him sit up straight.

"It's Nakshatra Resort."

Nakshatra. The name felt oddly familiar. It stirred something in his memory, but he couldn't quite place it.

Aniket stared at the screen, lost in thought. Why did that name feel so… known?

Chapter 14
Knowing

As soon as Sitara walked in, Anni felt something shift inside him—an excitement he couldn't afford to show. He leaned back on the couch, pretending to be indifferent.

"How was your day, Tara?" he asked casually.

She narrowed her eyes. "I told you not to call me Tara," she huffed.

Anni smirked, but before he could tease her further, he noticed something—an exhaustion in her eyes, a weight she carried. He had an odd urge to take that weight away, to make sure she never had to carry anything heavy alone.

"Fine," he said, leaning forward. "How was your day?"

"Okay…" she murmured, hesitating. "And hurting too."

Something in her voice made his chest tighten. But instead of pressing, he changed the topic.

"Do you want to know more about me?" His voice was softer now.

Sitara raised a brow. "Of course," she said, intrigued, and settled into the chair across from him.

For a moment, he lost himself. The way her golden-brown eyes gleamed under the dim light, how the stray strands of her front-cut hair fell perfectly over her face—it was a sight that made time slow down.

She snapped her fingers. "Come on, Anni."

He cleared his throat, breaking free from the spell she unknowingly cast on him.

"I'm an orphan," he began, his voice steady but distant. "I grew up in Ashraya until 6th grade. Then, a woman took me in. I never called her 'Mom.'"

Sitara's face changed. "Ashraya?" she repeated. "I know that place."

A strange chill ran down his spine.

"They used to get food from Nakshatra Resort," she continued, thinking out loud. "We were one of their major donors."

Everything clicked at once.

Anni's hands clenched into fists. "So, everything from Nakshatra… went to Ashraya?"

She nodded slowly.

A wave of emotions hit him like a forgotten lullaby suddenly remembered in the dead of night. The hands that once fed him, the place that sheltered him, the unseen force that kept him from falling apart—it all led back to her. To Sitara.

Maybe destiny had been weaving their stories together long before they had even spoken a word to each other.

"Okay, okay, tell me about your mom," Sitara said, her voice gentle.

Anni took a deep breath. "She was organized, strict… and lovely," he admitted. "She had a beautiful garden on the terrace. Roses, Tulsi, jasmine… She believed a home isn't a home without plants."

Sitara smiled faintly. "She sounds wonderful."

"She was," Anni whispered, then paused. "But she left me before my graduation."

Sitara frowned. "Left? You mean…"

"She died." The words felt heavier than they ever had before. "Blood cancer. On the same day she adopted me."

Sitara gasped, but she didn't speak. She just listened, her eyes reflecting an empathy he hadn't seen in anyone before.
"I regret calling her 'Ma'am' instead of 'Mom,'" Anni continued, staring at the floor. "But she never minded. She just wanted me to succeed. She always told me…

'Love isn't in what you call me, it's in what you become because of me.'"

A lump formed in his throat, but he swallowed it down.

Sitara's eyes shimmered. "She would be so proud of you," she whispered.

He exhaled, a ghost of a smile on his lips.

"When you mentioned Nakshatra," he said finally, looking at her, "I felt like I already knew you… even before I saw you."

And in that moment, Sitara realized—sometimes, the universe doesn't introduce two people when they meet. It introduces them when their souls recognize each other.

Chapter 15
New Friendships & Secrets

The sky outside was painted in deep hues of orange and purple as Saanvi paced around her room, her phone pressed against her ear. She tapped her foot impatiently, waiting for the familiar voice on the other end.

"Ugh, Anni is not picking up. Is he home?" she asked the moment Sitara answered the call.

Sitara, lounging lazily on her couch, raised an eyebrow. "Uh, no? Is something important?"

"Not really," Saanvi sighed. "Just needed to talk to him. Where is he?"

"Probably in his office or in court. You know how he is," Sitara replied, scrolling through her phone absentmindedly.

The conversation drifted from Aniket to random topics—latest fashion trends, celebrity gossip, and the struggles of finding a good coffee shop that didn't burn their espresso. Eventually, Saanvi ended the call with a casual, "Talk later."

Later That Evening

When Aniket finally returned home, exhausted from the weight of another long day, Sitara greeted him with a smirk as he loosened his tie.

"Oh, by the way, Saanvi called me today, asking if you were home," she mentioned casually, watching his reaction.

Aniket, mid-way through shrugging off his blazer, raised an eyebrow.
"And?"

Sitara leaned back on the couch, folding her arms.
"And let me tell you something interesting—she didn't call because she was worried about you."

Aniket chuckled, curiosity flashing in his eyes.
"Then why did she call?"

Sitara tilted her head, a playful glint in her eyes.
"Because she wanted to bond with me. She liked my vibe that day and wants to be my friend."

Aniket let out a soft laugh, shaking his head.
"She's trying to recruit you as her girl bestie?"

"Exactly." Sitara nodded. "She doesn't have many close friends except me. And as long as I've known her, she's always wanted a girl best friend. That's why she reached out."
Aniket smirked.
"So, basically, she's adopting you."

Sitara rolled her eyes.
"Oh, and don't get any weird ideas. She already has a boyfriend."

Aniket raised an eyebrow.
"Does Chintu know this?"

A mischievous grin spread across Sitara's face.
"No. And don't tell him either—it'll ruin his flirting practice."

Aniket burst into laughter, shaking his head.
"Poor guy."

Later That Night

Sitara lay in bed, staring at the ceiling, the glow of her bedside lamp casting long shadows on the walls. A strange thought settled in her mind.

"This is… different," she mused. "I mean, Mom used to be my best friend. We'd talk about everything—clothes, gossip, life. But now… I don't have that anymore."

She sighed, rolling onto her side, her fingers hovering over her phone.

"Maybe it's okay to be Saanvi's friend. Let's give it a try." Without overthinking, she picked up her phone and sent Saanvi a girly meme.

Across the City

Saanvi, curled up in bed, scrolling through her messages, saw the notification pop up.

A meme. From Sitara.

A slow smirk crept onto her face as she read it.

"Well, well, well… looks like I've got myself a bestie."

She quickly typed back a response, something sarcastic yet playful, something that fit the rhythm of their newfound connection.

And just like that, a new friendship was born.

Chapter 16
Don't Judge! (Or do?)

The café smelled of fresh coffee and mild arrogance. It was the kind of place where cappuccinos came with delicate foam art, and conversations dripped with both caffeine and sass.

Saanvi and Sitara sat across from Aniket, their eyes glinting with mischief. Aniket, ever the picture of composed professionalism, scrolled through his phone, feigning ignorance to the silent war of glances his two friends were exchanging.

Saanvi leaned forward, resting her chin on her palm.
"So, Mr. Lawyer, how does it feel getting paid to argue all day?"

Sitara gasped dramatically, nearly spilling her coffee.
"Omg, do you wake up every morning and just pick a random person to yell 'Objection!' at?"

Aniket exhaled, finally looking up with a tired but amused expression.
"Oh, totally. Sometimes I even rehearse in front of the mirror. Gotta makes sure my dramatic pauses are courtroom ready."

Saanvi smirked.

"Makes sense. Do you also carry a tiny gavel in your pocket? You know, just in case?"

Sitara's gasp was even louder this time, her eyes widening in mock horror.
"Wait… Do you, like, secretly judge us? Just mentally scoring us while we talk?"

Aniket, sipping his coffee with unbearable calmness, pulled out his phone, tilted the screen slightly toward them, and made a show of pretending to present it to an invisible judge.
"I never judge," he said smoothly. "But Exhibit A begs to differ."

Saanvi and Sitara gasped in unison, exchanging dramatic looks.

"This is an attack," Sitara whispered.

"He's learning from us," Saanvi muttered.

Sitara shook her head, placing a hand over her heart as if deeply wounded.
"We created a monster."

Aniket leaned back, enjoying their melodrama.
"Oh please, if anyone here is putting on a performance, it's you two."

Saanvi raised a perfectly arched brow.
"Excuse me? Acting is an art."

Sitara flipped her hair, her voice dripping with mock sophistication.
"And influencing is hard work!"

Aniket's deadpan stare didn't waver.
"Right. Because spending three hours deciding between 'Golden Sunset' and 'Parisian Warmth' as an Instagram filter is exhausting."

Saanvi placed a hand over her chest.
"I feel personally attacked."

Sitara scoffed, crossing her arms.
"Oh yeah? At least we don't spend our time reading boring case files."

Aniket tilted his head slightly.
"Right, because memorizing fake scripts and recording twenty takes of the same 'casual laughter' video is totally more intellectual."

Sitara's jaw dropped.
"Okay, rude!"

"First of all," Saanvi interjected, pointing a well-manicured finger, "our job requires real talent."

"Yeah!" Sitara chimed in. "Do you have any idea how hard it is to look candid while selling protein powder?"
Aniket blinked.

"Right. True skill. Almost as hard as finding a new way to say, 'Hey guys, welcome back to my channel' every week."

Sitara gasped, clutching her coffee cup like it was a lifeline.
"You are NOT invited to our next brand trip."

Saanvi patted Aniket's arm, her tone dripping with fake sympathy.
"It's okay, buddy. Maybe one day you'll win a case as important as finding the perfect lighting setup."

Aniket rolled his eyes.
"You're right. I should quit law and start promoting sugar-free gummies with zero health benefits."

Saanvi and Sitara gasped as if he had insulted their ancestors.

"HOW DARE—"

Their dramatic outburst was cut short by the arrival of their coffees, the tension diffusing into the steam that curled lazily from their cups. But the damage was done. Aniket, the ever-composed legal mind, had won this round.

He took a slow, smug sip of his coffee, while Saanvi and Sitara sulked, already plotting their next move.
This war between professions was far from over.

Chapter 17
A Fishy Situation

The night before, Sitara had gone on and on about her early morning shoot, dramatically complaining about having to leave the house by 5 AM. Aniket, ever the skeptic of her self-discipline, had simply nodded along.

"5 AM? Sure," he had said, smirking. "I'll believe it when I see it."

But somehow, curiosity got the better of him.

So, the next morning, half an hour earlier than usual, he stepped out of his room just to check. And there she was—standing at the sink, toothbrush in hand, completely lost in sleep.

Except… she wasn't brushing her teeth.

Instead, she was moving her head—left, right, left, right—while the toothbrush remained frozen mid-air.

Aniket pressed a hand over his mouth, his shoulders shaking with silent laughter. How does she survive like this?

And as if on cue, in her half-conscious state, she clumsily stubbed her toe against the table leg.

"Ouch—ahh, my knee!" she groaned, rubbing her head instead.

Aniket sighed. This level of chaos should be illegal.

But, to her credit, she did what she said she would—by 5 AM sharp, she was out the door, miraculously awake, dressed, and ready for her shoot. Aniket watched her leave, a small smile lingering on his lips.

Maybe I should give her more credit.

He stretched lazily, walked into the hall, and absentmindedly glanced at the table in front of the TV.

Then he froze.
The fishbowl was empty.

Bittu was gone.

A sharp pang of realization hit him—Sitara would freak out if she saw this. She always said misfortunes followed her like a curse, and this? This would just reinforce her dramatic superstitions.

"No, no, no—I have to fix this before she gets back!"

Panic shot through him as he searched the floor, under the table, behind the books—until finally, his breath caught.

There, under the table, lay a tiny, glistening figure. Still. Silent.

Bittu.

Aniket didn't think. He dropped to his knees, scooping up the little fish with the gentleness of someone holding something impossibly fragile. His pulse quickened as he rushed to the sink, whispering,

"C'mon, buddy, you have to make it."

The house, just moments ago filled with laughter, now held a different kind of silence—the kind that came when something delicate was at stake.

He turned on the tap, cupping cool water in his palm and letting it trickle over Bittu's tiny form. Seconds stretched unbearably long.

And then—a faint, almost invisible twitch.

Aniket held his breath. Another twitch. A flick of the fin.

"Yes!" he whispered, almost giddy.

Moving quickly, he refilled the fishbowl and placed Bittu back inside, watching in relief as the tiny creature wobbled at first, then steadied itself, its golden tail swishing through the water once more.

Aniket exhaled, resting his hands on his knees.
"You nearly gave me a heart attack, You tiny menace."

Bittu, oblivious to the near-death experience, bobbed around in the water, as if nothing had happened.

Aniket ran a hand through his hair, shaking his head. Crisis averted. Barely.

But then, just as he was about to leave, another thought struck him.

Sitara could never know.

If she found out, she would go on for weeks about how her bad luck had almost murdered her pet. She would stage a full-blown dramatic funeral, force him to write a eulogy, and probably hold Bittu Appreciation Day every month to commemorate the "miracle."

Nope. She could not know.

So, he did the only thing he could—he wiped away every trace of evidence, adjusted the bowl to its exact original position, and casually strolled back to his room as if nothing had happened.
Bittu was fine.
The world was fine.
And Sitara would never know a thing.

Unless, of course, Bittu decided to snitch.
Aniket paused at his door, throwing one last glance at the fishbowl.

"Stay quiet, buddy. This stays between us."

Bittu swished his tail.

Traitor.

Chapter 18
Love, Unspoken

It started as a whisper, a flicker in the quiet.
A name lingering too long on his lips, a glance stolen without meaning to.

Sitara.

Aniket didn't know when it happened—only that it had.
Maybe it was in the way she twirled a spoon absentmindedly when lost in thought.
Or the way she'd gasp in horror when her eyeliner smudged—like the world had truly wronged her.
Maybe it was the way she cursed her own clumsiness yet danced through chaos like it was choreographed for her alone.

Maybe it was everything.

And the realization sat heavy in his chest.
Loving her was not the problem.
The problem was what now?

The only person he could say it to—the only one who would understand—was Saanvi.
So, one evening, as the sun melted into hues of quiet gold, he sat across from her, fingers drumming against the table, words itching to break free.

"I think… I have feelings for Sitara."

Saanvi stilled. Then, slowly, a smirk curled her lips.

"You think?" she scoffed. "Anni, please. I knew it the moment you stopped making fun of her twenty retakes for a single video."

Aniket frowned. Had it been that obvious?

But Saanvi wasn't done. She leaned in, eyes dancing with delight.

"How didn't you fall for her? Have you seen her? She looks like a painting, for God's sake—every expression, every little frown, like an artist's unfinished masterpiece. So beautiful, so humble, so full of love—Anni, you had to fall. It was just a matter of when."

Aniket let out a breathless chuckle, shaking his head.

"You make it sound like I never had a choice."

Saanvi shrugged. "Did you?"

And no. He didn't.
Sitara had waltzed into his life, in all her sleepy, chaotic, breathtaking glory, and she had stayed.
She had filled spaces he didn't know were empty.
She had become a part of him so effortlessly that he never noticed—until now.

"So," Saanvi folded her arms, eyes gleaming with mischief. "What now? Are you going to tell her? Keep it a secret? Or just… suffer?"

Aniket sighed, leaning back, staring at the ceiling as if it held answers.

"I don't know."

Because what if she didn't feel the same?
What if she laughed it off?
What if he lost her—not as a lover, but as a friend?
Loving her in silence was safer.
But was it enough?

Saanvi watched him for a moment before tilting her head.

"You know, Anni… Some stories are meant to be written in whispers. But some? Some demand to be spoken aloud."

The question remained. Which one was theirs?

Chapter 19
A War Zone of Love

The house had always been a battleground—
A place where cushions became weapons, sarcasm became shields, and stolen snacks declared war.

Today was no different. Except, for Aniket, everything was different.

Because today, in every little moment, he felt himself falling more.

The Breakfast Battle

"This toast is burnt." Sitara wrinkled her nose, holding up the slightly charred bread.

"It's golden brown," Aniket corrected.

"Golden brown? Anni, this is the same color as my failed eyeliner attempts!"

Aniket smirked, taking a bite from his own toast. "Then maybe your eyeliner skills need help, not my toast."

Sitara gasped in mock offense. "Wow. That was a personal attack."
She crossed her arms, pouting. And damn it, why did she have to look cute while being mad?

"Fine. I'll eat it." She took a dramatic bite, chewing slowly. Then, looking him dead in the eye, she grabbed his coffee and took a sip.

Aniket froze. That was his coffee. His cup.

Sitara didn't even flinch.

"Horrible toast deserves good coffee," she said with a smirk.

And Aniket, instead of being annoyed, just watched her— thinking how unfair it was that someone could steal both his coffee and his heart in a single moment.

The Pillow Fight Truce

It started, as always, with Sitara stealing the TV remote.

"You always watch boring law stuff," she whined.

"And you always watch cringe influencers pretending their lives are perfect," he shot back.

Sitara narrowed her eyes. "Take that back."

"Make me."

One second later, a pillow hit him in the face.
A full-blown war erupted feathers flying, laughter echoing, each of them launching attacks like warriors in battle. But somewhere between dodging a particularly

aggressive throw and tackling her onto the couch—his heart skipped a beat.

She was inches away, breathless, eyes shining with amusement.

"I win," she whispered, holding the remote like a trophy.

And Aniket, looking at her, thought—
If this is losing, I never want to win.

The 'Accidental' Touches

It was the smallest things that hit him hardest.

The way she'd brush past him in the hallway, her fingers lightly grazing his arm.
The way she'd grab his hand absentmindedly while scrolling through something funny on her phone.
The way her laughter filled the house—like sunlight, like home.

Every touch, every glance, every little fight—he was falling.
And today, he was falling faster.

The Nighttime Realization
By night, the house had settled, the battles had ended.
Sitara, curled up on the couch, was watching some old movie. Aniket sat nearby, pretending to read but really just watching her.

How was she so unaware of the way she affected him?

The way she hugged a pillow while watching?
The way she hummed along to the movie's music.
The way she was just… herself?

And maybe, just maybe—this wasn't a war zone after all.
Maybe it was a battlefield he had already surrendered to.

Because today, in every argument, every laugh, every
stupid fight—Aniket realized something.

Loving Sitara wasn't something that happened.

Loving her was something he did.

Every second, every moment.

And the real war?

The war was within him—
To tell her. Or to keep falling in silence.

Chapter 20
Strawberries

It started with a plant.
A tiny, delicate strawberry plant—a gift, a gesture, a memory wrapped in green.

Sitara placed it on the table with a proud grin.
"To make this house feel like home for you, Anni."

Aniket blinked at her, something warm blooming in his chest.
"You remembered."

She scoffed. "Of course. I remember everything."
The Battle of the Perfect Spot

But of course, their peace lasted all of five minutes.

"It should go near the window—sunlight, you know?" Aniket said, placing it near the sill.

"No, no. It belongs in the kitchen! It'll be so cute there!" Sitara insisted, moving it again.

"Kitchen? So, it can hear your dramatic monologues while cooking? Poor thing will die of stress."

"Excuse me? My cooking is divine!"

The plant moved from window to kitchen to balcony, then back again, traveling like a lost suitcase at an airport.

Then Aniket, being his usual over-the-top self, pulled out a piece of paper.
"Fine. Since you're impossible, I present to you—a watering timetable."

Sitara stared at it.
"You actually made a schedule? Anni, this is next-level nerd behavior."

"Unlike you, I believe in structure."

"Structure my foot, this is a dictatorship! Do I need to sign somewhere? Give a thumb impression?"

Aniket smirked. "Would you like a contract too? Maybe some legal jargon?"

Sitara rolled her eyes, climbed onto the sofa to escape his nonsense, and—

—slipped.
The Fall (And the First Touch of Something More)

It happened fast.

A gasp. A twisted ankle. A sharp pain shooting up her leg.

"Owwww!" Sitara clutched her foot, wincing. "Anni, I think—ow—it's really bad."

Aniket, already kneeling beside her, frowned. "You always exaggerate—" Then he saw her face, her hands trembling slightly. His heart did a strange flip. "Okay, okay. No sarcasm. Let's get you to a hospital."

Sitara nodded. Then tried to stand.

Only to almost fall again.

"Umm. I...I can't walk."

Aniket exhaled. "Well, guess there's only one solution."

He moved closer, bent down slightly, and—

Lifted her.

Just like that.

Sitara let out a tiny yelp as her arms instinctively looped around his neck.

Her heart pounded. His grip was firm, careful, warm.

It was the first time he had ever held her like this. And suddenly, the entire world tilted—not because of her ankle, but because of him.

"Anni—"
"Shhh. Let me enjoy this. It's not every day I get to carry a human-sized drama queen."

She swatted his shoulder. "You're impossible."

"And you're light. Are you even eating properly?"

"Put me down, I changed my mind!"

"Nope. You literally can't walk. And honestly, this moment is too cinematic to ruin."

He was teasing—but beneath it, his voice was softer, almost... different.

Their eyes met. For the first time, there was no war. No witty comeback.

Just silence.
Just them.

And for the first time, Sitara had no idea how to fight it.

The Aftermath (Or, Aniket's Revenge)

The trip to the hospital was straight out of a rom-com.
She sat in the car, blushing for no reason, stealing glances at him.
He drove like he wasn't affected at all, but his grip on the steering wheel told another story.

It was almost perfect.

Until they came back home.

"Okay, great. Now, don't even think about carrying me back—" Sitara declared, trying to step out of the car.

Aniket smirked. A dangerous smirk.

"Oh, don't worry, Princess Sitara. I won't carry you."

A second later, he pulled something from the back seat—

A wheelchair.

Sitara froze. "You did NOT just—"

"Oh, but I did." Aniket unfolded it like a villain unveiling his master plan. "Since you refuse to be carried, I had to get creative."

"Anni, I swear—"

"Come, come. Let me roll you to your throne."
Sitara groaned. "You're enjoying this, aren't you?"

"Immensely."

He placed her in the chair like a true gentleman—and then ran with it.

Sitara screamed. "ANIKET!"

"Wheeeeee—" He pushed it like they were in an action movie. "Fast and Furious: Wheelchair Drift Edition!"

"I will MURDER you."

"Aww, but you're smiling."

And damn it. She was.

Even as she yelled, even as she pretended to be mad, she was laughing—loud, unfiltered, like nothing in the world mattered.
Aniket, watching her, knew one thing for sure.

He had fallen.

Again.

And there was no coming back.

Chapter 21
Caregivers

It was just a twisted ankle.
Not a war. Not a tragedy.
But Aniket, in all his over-the-top glory, made it a national emergency.

He called for reinforcements.

First came Saanvi—camera in hand, excitement in her eyes.
"Oh my God, Sitara, say hi to your fans!" she grinned, flipping her phone toward Sitara.

Sitara groaned. "Saanvi, I am injured, not famous."

"Well, you look like both."

And then, of course, came Chintu—because what's chaos without him?
"Saanvi, do you believe in love at first sight?" he asked dramatically, plopping onto the couch beside her.

Saanvi smirked. "I believe in blocking at first text."

"Ouch, woman. My heart."

Sitara laughed despite herself. The house, once filled with pain and sulking, was alive again—

A whirlwind of banter, laughter, and chaos.

And in between it all—
Aniket.

"Careful, careful—your highness must not strain herself,"
Aniket teased, adjusting the pillow beneath her foot.

Sitara rolled her eyes. "You do realize it's just a sprain,
right? Not a royal decree?"

"You wouldn't know. You act like a queen all the time."

"And you act like my personal butler."

"Glad you finally see it." He smirked. "Now, shall I fetch
your grapes, Your Grace?"
She swatted at him, but he dodged effortlessly. And yet—
Every time he touched her, even casually—
To fix her pillow.
To adjust her bandage.
To hand her a glass of water—

His fingers lingered. Not long enough to notice, but long
enough to feel.

And his eyes.

She started seeing it then.

The way they softened when she laughed.

The way they flickered, like holding back words he couldn't say.
The way they rested on her, just a second too long.

Her mind told her it was nothing.
But her heart—
Her heart was beginning to understand.

"Alright, guys, this is the part where we test how much Sitara can tolerate before she throws something at me!" Saanvi grinned, still vlogging.

"Saanvi, I swear, put that away before I—"

"Before you what? Hobble over and stop me?"

Aniket laughed—really laughed, and the sound sent a strange warmth through Sitara's chest.

And just then, Saanvi turned the camera toward him.

"So, Aniket, tell the world—how does it feel to be Sitara's personal nurse?"

He smirked, but there was something undeniably tender in his voice when he answered.

"Exhausting. She's the most stubborn patient alive."

Sitara stuck out her tongue. "You're the one who called for backup."

"I had to. Otherwise, you'd try to run a marathon with a sprained ankle."

"Oh please, I—"

And then, suddenly—

Saanvi flipped the screen back toward Sitara.

"Ooooh, girl. You need to see how he looks at you when you're not watching."

Sitara's heart skipped. "W-What?"

Aniket, for the first time, stumbled. "Saanvi—stop being dramatic."

Saanvi smirked. "I don't have to be. The camera doesn't lie."

Sitara swallowed. She didn't check the footage.
She didn't need to.

Because she had started seeing it for herself.

And suddenly, her ankle wasn't the only thing that twisted

Chapter 22
The Sudden Confession

It started like every other argument—
Fire and ice, laughter and war.

"Anni, we are having a movie night."
"Tara, we are not having a movie night."

"Why not?" she huffed, arms crossed.
"Because I said so."
"Oh, I didn't know we lived in a dictatorship now."

Aniket sighed, rubbing his temples. "Tara, I just—"
"I am injured, Anni. How can you refuse a wounded soul?" she interrupted, dramatically clutching her ankle like a tragic heroine.

"Oh, don't even start—"
"You heartless monster! I am weak, in pain, suffering—"

He groaned. "You twisted your ankle, not fought a war."

"Same thing."

Aniket rolled his eyes. "Fine, fine! One movie. But nothing emotional."

"A romance, then!"

"Tara, no."

"Tara, yes!"

"Tara, I swear—"

And then she grinned—that grin. The one that meant trouble.

"If you don't agree, Anni, I will kill you."

And maybe it was exhaustion. Maybe it was fate.
Or maybe Aniket had held it in for too long.

Because before he could stop himself, he whispered—

"Then love me, Tara."
Silence.

The air shifted; the world paused.

She blinked. "W-What?"

"Love me," he repeated, voice steady, eyes burning into hers.

She stared at him, caught between disbelief and something unspoken.

And then—
"Nah."

A smirk, a shrug, a casual dismissal—
But this time, he didn't let it slip away.

Aniket leaned forward, close enough that she could hear the quiet storm in his breath.
"You took too long to say no, Tara."

She swallowed. "So?"

"So, don't lie to me." His voice softened, but his eyes held her captive.
"Don't say it's nothing. Don't pretend you don't feel it, too."

Her heart pounded against her ribs. "Anni—"

"You always said if you love someone, they'll die." His fingers curled gently around her wrist, a touch that was both a question and an answer.
"If loving you is a death sentence, then let it be."

Her breath hitched. "Don't say things like that."

"Why not?" His voice dropped lower, deeper.
"It's been months, Tara. Months of trying to ignore it, of waiting for you to see it, of holding back when all I wanted was to—"

He stopped himself.

Because he knew.

He could see it now—in her eyes, in the way she hadn't pulled away.
She had already fallen.

Maybe she always had.

And for the first time, Sitara had nothing to say.

Chapter 23
The Breakup

Saanvi sat on the couch, hugging a pillow, her eyes red and puffy. "He broke up with me!" she wailed. "Just like that! Over a text! A TEXT, Anni! Who does that?!"

Aniket, standing beside her with his arms crossed, looked ready to set someone on fire. "That good-for-nothing idiot! If I ever see him, I swear I'll—"

"Tell him you love him too?" Chintu entered dramatically, holding a half-eaten apple. "Because clearly, you care way too much."
Aniket glared at him. "Chintu, not now."

But Chintu wasn't one to back down. He took another bite of his apple and turned to Saanvi. "Wait a second—hold up! Saanvi had a boyfriend?! Since when? Nobody told me!" He dramatically clutched his heart. "I have been flirting with a taken woman this whole time. All my skills… wasted! I feel so betrayed."

Saanvi wiped her nose with the sleeve of her sweater. "Chintu, not the time."

"Not the time? It's exactly the time! I need closure. I need a moment to grieve! Do you know how much effort I put into my smooth lines? All for NOTHING!"

Anni sighed, patting his shoulder. "Chintu don't worry. You can start all over again. You have a shot now."

Chintu gasped. "Oh my God. You're right. It's a fresh start!" He turned back to Saanvi. "So… do you want to fall in love at first sight or should I walk by again?"

Saanvi threw a cushion at him. "Shut up, Chintu!"

As the chaos unfolded, Sitara sat silently on the edge of the couch. She wasn't reacting to anything.
But her eyes…

They were locked onto his.

Across the room, he was watching her too. Neither said a word, yet a thousand conversations seemed to pass between them. The stolen glances. The unsaid thoughts. The weight of unspoken emotions.

Saanvi, despite being heartbroken, was not blind. She nudged Anni, whispering, "Why are they staring at each other like that? Is there a telepathic war going on?"

Anni smirked. "Nah. That's what happens when two people have things left unsaid."

Chintu, oblivious as always, waved a hand in front of Sitara's face. "Hello? Earth to Sitara? You okay? Or are you buffering?"
Sitara blinked, breaking the moment. "Huh? Yeah. I mean—what?"

Chintu looked between her and him, squinting suspiciously. "Ohhhh. Something's fishy. Very fishy."

Anni patted Chintu's back. "Focus, man. Your mission is to make Saanvi laugh."

Chintu immediately went into action. "Saanvi, what's the best way to get over a breakup?"

"I don't know."

"Date me."

Another pillow came flying at his face.

The room filled with laughter, but amidst it all, Sitara sat there, still feeling his gaze on her. Still knowing that things had changed. And yet, pretending as if they hadn't.

Chapter 24
The Getaway

Sitara leaned against the kitchen counter, watching Saanvi poke at her untouched cup of chai. The breakup had taken a toll on her, and Sitara wasn't going to sit back and let her sulk any longer.

"That's it," Sitara declared. "We're going to the resort." Saanvi blinked. "What?"

"You need a break, and what better place than my father's resort? Fresh air, good food, and no phone calls from losers who don't deserve you."

"I don't know, Sitara—"

"Oh, I do," Chintu interrupted, appearing out of nowhere. "And I second this idea. I mean, who says no to a free resort stay?"

Saanvi sighed. "I never invited you."

Chintu clutched his chest dramatically. "That hurts, Saanvi. But don't worry, I have already RSVP'd."

Sitara smirked. "Well, if Chintu's coming, then I guess Aniket will have no choice but to tag along."
Aniket, who had just entered the room, frowned. "Excuse me?"

Chintu patted his back. "Don't fight it, bro. We all know if Sitara says something, it's happening."

Aniket sighed. "I have work."

"And I have an emotional support friend who needs cheering up," Sitara countered. "So, pack your bags, big-shot lawyer. We leave tomorrow."

The drive to the resort was filled with Chintu's constant commentary and Saanvi's vlogging. She refused to let her audience miss out on her 'healing journey,' as she called it. Sitara rolled her eyes but smiled—at least Saanvi was showing some signs of normalcy.

As they arrived, the grandeur of Sitara's family resort took Aniket by surprise. He had seen pictures but being there in person was a different feeling altogether. The warm tones of the wooden structures, the lush greenery, and the aroma of fresh flowers gave the place a nostalgic charm.

Chintu stretched his arms. "Ahh, this is the life! Five-star treatment, a pool, and unlimited food. I might never leave."

Sitara rolled her eyes. "You were never invited to stay permanently."

They settled in, but as Aniket walked around the resort, a particular room caught his attention. Unlike the rest of the open, airy spaces, this one was closed off, the wooden doors firmly shut, with a sign that read **'No Entry.'**

Curiosity sparked in him. "What's in there?" he asked Sitara.

She stiffened. "It's my father's room. No one goes in."

Aniket noted the change in her demeanor but didn't press further. Instead, he let the thought linger. What memories did this room hold, and why was it off-limits?

Later that evening, as the group gathered for dinner under the soft glow of lanterns, the air buzzed with laughter and conversation. The resort's chef had prepared a traditional South Indian feast—steaming idlis, crispy dosas, and fragrant coconut chutney. Chintu, of course, had taken it upon himself to try everything on the table.

"Saanvi, tell your vlog followers that this is the best food in the world," he said, stuffing his mouth with another bite of vada. "If I ever get married, I want my wedding feast to be exactly like this."

Saanvi rolled her eyes. "You first need someone willing to marry you."

Chintu gasped, placing a dramatic hand over his heart. "Sitara, did you hear that? My self-esteem has been shattered beyond repair."
Sitara smirked. "You had self-esteem?"
As the teasing continued, Aniket found himself watching Sitara. The way she laughed, the way she effortlessly played along with Chintu's antics—it was something he

hadn't noticed before. Or maybe he had, but only now was it making his heart race.

"Anni, you're staring," Saanvi whispered, smirking.

Aniket cleared his throat. "I'm not."

"Oh, you totally are," she teased. "What's stopping you? Too scared to admit you like her?"

Before Aniket could respond, Chintu clapped his hands. "Alright, folks! Since we're at a fancy resort, I say we do something thrilling! Let's sneak into that 'No Entry' room and see what's inside."

Sitara's expression immediately darkened. "Absolutely not."

Chintu blinked. "Why not? What's in there, a treasure chest?"

"No. It's private." Her voice held finality, but Aniket could see the flicker of emotion in her eyes.

Chintu huffed. "Fine, fine. No breaking and entering. But at least tell us why it's off-limits."

Sitara looked away, her fingers gripping the edge of the table. "Because it holds everything that once made this place home."

The table fell into silence.

Aniket wanted to say something, to reach out. But before he could, Chintu broke the tension as only he could.

"Well," he said, picking up another vada. "If no one's breaking into secret rooms, can we at least break into the dessert section?"
Laughter filled the air again, but Aniket knew that the room—and the emotions tied to it—weren't something Sitara could ignore forever. And maybe, just maybe, he would be the one to help her face it.

Chapter 25
Unspoken Truths

The resort had gone quiet, with only the distant chirping of crickets filling the night air. Aniket tossed and turned in bed, but sleep refused to come. His thoughts kept drifting back to that locked room, to Sitara's reaction, to the weight it seemed to carry.

Unable to resist his curiosity, he quietly slipped out of his room and made his way down the dimly lit corridor. As he stood before the closed door, he exhaled, running his fingers over the old wood. What was behind it that held so much of Sitara's past?

"You won't find answers by just staring at it," a soft voice said behind him.

He turned to find Sitara standing there, arms crossed, her expression unreadable.

Aniket hesitated. "I wasn't trying to sneak in or anything. I just... I can't stop thinking about it."

She studied him for a moment before sighing. "Come," she said, unlocking the door. "I'll show you."

The room was pristine, carefully preserved. Photographs adorned the walls—Sitara as a child, dancing, swimming, skating. A small frock hung on the wall, perfectly framed. In the corner, there was a shelf filled with trinkets, memories of a childhood long gone.

Aniket looked around in awe. "Your father must have loved you unconditionally. This single room shows it." Sitara's eyes shimmered. "He did."

As Aniket wandered, his gaze landed on a particular photograph. A tiny Sitara, fresh out of a shower, wrapped in a dark blue towel, droplets of water still clinging to her face. She was laughing, the kind of pure, unfiltered joy that made something tighten in his chest.

Without thinking, he took the photo. Sitara noticed but said nothing.

"Enough of exploring," she said, wiping her eyes. "Let's go."

But Aniket knew he had seen something that mattered—something that made him want to protect that joy in her forever.

The trip to the resort had been refreshing for everyone. Saanvi felt a sense of relief, as if a weight had been lifted off her shoulders. Chintu and Aniket, on the other hand, had the time of their lives, laughing, playing, and making memories they would cherish. It had been one of those rare moments when everything felt perfect—carefree and full of joy.

But while the trip had ended, some things remained unchanged.

On the 29th of every month, Sitara made it a point to visit the resort. It had become a tradition of hers, something she never missed. No matter where she was or how busy she got, she always found time to return, overseeing everything personally. It wasn't just about managing the place—it was something deeper, something personal.

Once they returned to their apartment, they lingered for a moment before saying their goodbyes. The atmosphere was light-hearted, with Chintu still caught up in the excitement of their trip. He couldn't resist teasing Sitara about her wealth.

"I still don't get it," he said, shaking his head in exaggerated disbelief. "You own a whole resort, yet you live in this tiny apartment? What's the deal, Sitara? You could be living in a palace!"

Aniket chuckled at Chintu's antics, while Saanvi simply smiled. But Sitara's expression changed. The teasing, though harmless, touched upon something she rarely spoke about.

Everyone had wondered at some point—why did she choose to live in such a modest place when she could afford so much more? The answer was simple, yet difficult to say aloud. It wasn't about money. It wasn't about luxury. It was about escaping the ghosts of her past.

Loneliness had crept into her life like an unwelcome guest, and the memories she tried to bury still followed her wherever she went. The resort was a reminder of things she had lost, and staying there only made the pain resurface.

Whenever the conversation steered in that direction, Sitara would go silent. Her usual confidence would waver, and for a moment, she would seem lost in thoughts she didn't want to revisit.

Saanvi noticed it first, then Chintu, who immediately regretted bringing it up.

But before the silence could stretch too long, Aniket stepped in, as he always did.

"Alright, enough about that," he said with a grin, his voice deliberately cheerful. "Who's up for some ice cream? I'm treating. But you only get one scoop, Chintu—no way I'm letting you rob me blind."

The distraction worked. Chintu immediately jumped at the opportunity to argue about how one scoop was an insult to his appetite, and just like that, the heaviness in the air faded.

Sitara shot Aniket a grateful glance but said nothing. She didn't have to.

The night went on, filled with casual conversations and laughter.

But deep down, they all knew—some things were better left unspoken.

Chapter 26
Short romance

That night, sleep eluded Aniket. No matter how much he tossed and turned, he couldn't find peace. His thoughts were restless, lingering on things he didn't quite understand—on her. Sitara.

With a sigh, he gave up trying to sleep and decided to step out for some air. As he walked past Sitara's room, he noticed something unusual—her door was slightly ajar, and the soft glow of the bedside lamp spilled into the hallway.

Curious, he hesitated for a moment before gently pushing the door open. To his surprise, the door wasn't locked.

Inside, Sitara lay curled up on the bed, lost in sleep. Her hair cascaded over the pillow, framing her face in soft waves. The warm glow of the lamp highlighted her delicate features—her slightly parted lips, the gentle rise and fall of her chest, the peaceful expression that replaced the usual sharpness in her eyes.

Aniket stood there, watching her. He wasn't sure why, but he couldn't look away. She looked different when she slept—so vulnerable, so unguarded. She stirred slightly, shifting in her sleep, one hand sliding under her cheek. Then, as if sensing his presence, she stilled.

Seconds stretched between them, and just when he thought she had drifted back into deep sleep, she spoke— her voice drowsy yet teasing.

"You shouldn't stare at someone sleeping for this long."

Aniket smirked, leaning against the doorframe. "Then why did you get still and make it easier for me to stare?"

Sitara didn't open her eyes, but he saw the slight curve of her lips—an amused yet sleepy smile. And then, just as he was about to step back, he noticed it. The soft blush that crept onto her cheeks, even in the dim light.

A warmth spread through his chest at the sight. He took a step closer, lowering his voice to a whisper. "You know… you look different when you sleep."

She hummed lazily, turning her face slightly into the pillow, hiding that soft smile. "How?"

"Less fierce. More…" He paused, searching for the right word. "More like the girl who pretends she's not afraid of anything but really is."

Her breathing hitched slightly, but she said nothing. Maybe she didn't have a reply, or maybe she didn't want to find one.

After a few moments, Aniket let out a quiet chuckle and straightened. "Sleep, Sitara. You can scold me in the morning."

She didn't respond, but the way her lips pressed together told him she was still listening. He turned to leave, but just as he reached the door, he heard her murmur—so soft, he almost missed it.

"Goodnight, Anni."

He stopped. His heart did something strange at the sound of his name from her lips, said in a way no one else ever had.

"Goodnight, Sitara," he whispered back before closing the door behind him.

And as he walked away, he realized—he wasn't restless anymore.

Chapter 27
Bike ride

The morning air was crisp as they got ready to leave. Sitara adjusted her watch when Aniket suddenly asked, "Do you want me to drop you?"

She paused, turning to him with raised eyebrows. "This is strange… this is the first time you've ever asked me this."

Aniket shrugged, stuffing his hands into his pockets. "Felt like asking."

She smirked. "That's rude. At least ask in a way that makes me want to come with you."

He rolled his eyes but played along, leaning slightly toward her. "Princess Sitara, would you do me the honor of allowing me to escort you?" He even made a little bow.

She chuckled, shaking her head. "Better. But I still need motivation."
Aniket sighed dramatically before flashing his trump card. "I'm taking the Vespa."

Her eyes lit up instantly. Without a second thought, she blurted out, "Yes! But I'm riding it."

Amused, Aniket crossed his arms. "Are you sure? That means I'd have to sit on the backseat."

Sitara grinned, grabbing the keys from his hand. "You okay with that?"

He blinked at her, pretending to hesitate. "Not really."

"Too bad," she smirked and strutted toward the Vespa like she had just won a grand prize.

Aniket sighed but followed, hopping onto the backseat as she started the engine. The moment they hit the road; Sitara let out a happy sigh.

"My mom never let me ride bikes," she admitted, gripping the handles with excitement.

Aniket, holding onto the sides, smirked. "Well, now you can."

She turned slightly, giving him a sharp glance. "That's the second time you've said something like that."

"Like what?" he asked, feigning innocence.

"Like you're giving me things I was never allowed to have."

Aniket just smirked but didn't respond. That smirk alone made her want to wipe it off his face.

So, without warning, she hit the brakes hard.
Aniket lurched forward slightly but steadied himself almost immediately. Instead of panicking like she

expected, he just laughed. "Nice try, but you can't make me regret riding with you."

Sitara huffed. "Ugh, keep a distance from me!"

He leaned in slightly, voice low and teasing. **"Make me."**

She gulped, gripping the handle a little tighter. Her heartbeat sped up, but she refused to let him have the upper hand.

"Fine," she smirked. "Hold on tight."

And with that, she hit the accelerator, the Vespa speeding forward as Aniket laughed behind her, completely unbothered.

Little did she know, he was enjoying this ride for a whole different reason.

Chapter 28
Dream

After wrapping up his work for the day, Aniket dialled Sitara's number.

"Do you want to ride home with me?" he asked casually, expecting her usual excitement.

But her response came a little too soon. "Anni, I'm already home."

There was a pause, and she immediately noticed the hint of disappointment in his voice.

"Oh." He cleared his throat, trying to cover it up. "Okay then—what are you doing right now?"

Sitara smiled, sensing his mood shift. "Just cleaning Bittu's bowl and changing his water. Chatting with him a little."

Aniket chuckled. "Do you want to eat fish?"

She gasped. "ANIIIII!"

His laughter echoed through the phone. "Relax, I was joking! I meant for us, not for Bittu."
Sitara huffed. "You should be careful with your words. Bittu might take offense!"

"Right, right. I forgot he's royalty." Aniket teased. "Okay, tell me what you actually want to eat. I'll bring it home."

She thought for a moment before softly saying, "I want Ragi malt."

"Ragi malt?" he repeated, a little surprised.

"Yeah," she nodded. "Mom used to make it for me. It was my everyday breakfast for years."

Aniket smiled. "Oh, that's easy. I'll make it at home."

Sitara blinked. "Wait… you'll make it?"
"Yes, ma'am. Ragi isn't rich food for the world, but for the people of Karnataka, it's love. It deserves respect."

She grinned. "You're not wrong."

Half an hour later, Aniket arrived home, rolled up his sleeves, and got to work. He carefully stirred the ragi flour into boiling water, letting it thicken before pouring it into a bowl. When it was done, he placed it in front of her.
Sitara mixed it with milk and took a bite. The moment the familiar taste hit her tongue; she sighed in satisfaction. "This is so good."
Aniket watched her with amusement. "You really enjoy the small things in life, huh?"

She smiled, nodding. "I always have."
He leaned back against the chair, studying her. "Tell me about your unfinished dreams."

She went silent for a moment before looking at him with a soft smile. "I love the idea of being a mom. A really sweet little girl's mom." She chuckled. "When I was young, I always played with dolls, dressing them up in matching outfits, styling their hair the same way as mine. It was the cutest thing."

Aniket watched her with a gentle expression. "That's adorable."

She laughed. "And I want to act in a film. Not just any role, though—I want to play a character so unique and unforgettable that people remember the character's name more than the actress."

He tilted his head. "Like…?"

Her eyes lit up. "Do you know Deepa from *Paramatma*?"

Aniket nodded slowly.

"Something like that. A role so different, so special, that it stays with people forever. Or even a mythological character. I've always wanted to play one at least once."

Aniket smiled, seeing the passion in her eyes. "Those are beautiful dreams, Sitara."
She took another bite of her ragi malt and sighed happily. "And right now, my dream is to finish this bowl. Because it's *perfect*."

He laughed. "Well, then. Dream fulfilled."

She grinned. "One step at a time, Anni. One step at a time."

Chapter 29
Love you Bittu

Sitara sat near the fishbowl, her fingers gently tracing the glass as she whispered, "Love you, Bittu."

Bittu, the little gold fish, swam around gracefully, oblivious to the deep affection showered upon him. Sitara had always treated him like a family member, even going as far as not eating fish just to prove her loyalty.

Aniket, standing by the door with his arms crossed, smirked. "You know, it's weird that you say, 'love you' to a fish but never to me."

Sitara turned, narrowing her eyes. "That's because Bittu never cracks terrible jokes or calls me weird names."

Aniket gasped dramatically. "Oh, so I'm competing with a fish now?"

Sitara rolled her eyes. "Competing? Anni, you don't stand a chance. Bittu and I have a pure, unbreakable bond!"

Aniket scoffed. "Oh please, I love Bittu way more than you do. Who bought him? Me! Who cleans the tank when you 'forget'? Me! Who ensures he has fresh food? Again, me!"

Sitara crossed her arms. "Oh yeah? But who sings lullabies to him when he looks sad?"

Aniket blinked. "Wait… What? Sitara, he's a fish. He doesn't 'look sad.'"

Sitara gasped, covering Bittu's bowl with her hands. "Shhh! He can hear you, you heartless human!"

Aniket laughed. "Oh, come on! You're overreacting. Also, you're acting all loyal, but you eat fish! Hypocrisy at its finest."

Sitara placed her hands over her ears. "Lalala, I can't hear you. Also, I have *never* eaten fish in front of Bittu!"

Aniket smirked. "That's because he's always watching. The moment he's not there, you enjoy fish fry like there's no tomorrow."

Sitara pointed at him. "Take that back! Bittu is my best friend, and I would never betray him like that!"

Aniket shook his head. "You're being ridiculous. It's just a fish!"

Sitara gasped, her eyes widening in shock. "JUST. A. FISH?"

Aniket immediately regretted his words. "No, no, I didn't mean—"
But it was too late. Sitara, in her frustration, swung her hand toward him… except she miscalculated and— CRASH!!!

The fishbowl shattered. Water gushed onto the floor. And Bittu... poor, beloved Bittu, lay still.

Silence.

Sitara stared at the broken glass. "No... no, no, no, NO! Bittu! Speak to me! Swim! Do something!"

Aniket stood frozen. "Oh... my... god..."

They both dropped to the floor, frantically trying to save Bittu. Aniket gently nudged him. "Maybe he's just pretending? Maybe... maybe he's playing dead?"

Sitara glared at him with tears brimming in her eyes. "HE'S A FISH, ANNI! HE DOESN'T PRETEND!"

They cleaned the mess in complete silence. The house, which was filled with laughter moments ago, now felt unbearably heavy.

After everything was cleaned up, they both sat on the couch, staring at the empty space where Bittu's bowl once stood.

Aniket sighed. "I feel like we just committed a crime."

Sitara sniffed. "We did. We killed an innocent soul."

Aniket rubbed his face. "You killed him. Technically."

Sitara threw a pillow at him. "DON'T YOU DARE BLAME ME! IT WAS YOUR FAULT FOR CALLING HIM 'JUST A FISH'!"

Aniket sighed dramatically. "He died because of our love… we fought too much over him."

Sitara mumbled. "Love triangle gone wrong."

Silence stretched again. Then, after a few seconds, Sitara sniffled. "Anni… I miss him."

Aniket hesitated before gently patting her head. "I know, Tara. I know."

For the first time in a long time, she didn't mind him calling her Tara.

Chapter 30
Run

The room was dark, yet it wasn't the absence of light that made it unbearable—

It was the weight in her heart, the hollow ache that refused to fade.

Sitara sat on the bed, knees curled to her chest, her fingers digging into her arms.

Her breaths came out in shallow whispers, barely touching the air.

"It's my fault."

Her mind repeated the words like a cruel chant, each syllable sinking deeper into her soul.

She pressed her palms against her temples, trying to quiet the storm, but the voices inside screamed louder.

"What am I thinking? I left once. I started over. And yet, I'm doing the same mistake again."

She clenched her fists.

Her heart, once warm with love, now felt like a ticking bomb—ready to explode, ready to destroy everything she cherished.

"These people… If I love them, they will die. It's a curse I have."

Her chest tightened.

Bittu—her tiny, beautiful Bittu—was proof of it.

"The same day I told him I love him, he died."

A sob escaped her lips.

It wasn't just Bittu.

Anni.

Her mind whispered his name, and her whole body tensed.
"I'm going to lose him too."
Her fingers curled into the bedsheet, twisting it like she was trying to hold onto something—

but there was nothing to hold onto.

"Wait… what did I just say?

I'm going to lose Anni?
Does that mean…"

Her heart pounded against her ribcage.

She swallowed hard, blinking back the tears that blurred her vision.

"I love Anni."

The realization struck her like lightning, burning through her veins,
leaving her breathless, powerless.

Anni—her best friend, her worst fight, her only constant.

The one who made her laugh when she wanted to cry,
the one who made her argue when she wanted peace,
the one who… stayed.
And now…
She had to leave.

"Oh, Saanvi… Chintu… I can't play with people's lives anymore."

They mattered to her.
And that was the problem.

"I should leave them.

I should leave everything.

I should start over again."
But wasn't that what she had done before?
Hadn't she left once, hoping to erase the pain, only to find herself in the same agony again?

She gritted her teeth.

Running wouldn't change fate.

But staying…
"If I stay, I'll destroy them.

If I stay, I'll lose them.

If I stay…"

Tears rolled down her cheeks, warm and relentless.

She wiped them away angrily.
"No. Not this time.

Let me face it.

Let me not run."

Her whole body trembled.

It was a cruel choice—stay and risk losing them or leave and live with the ache forever.
"But wouldn't leaving be just another way of running away?"

She shook her head violently. "No. This is different. This is for them."
Her fingers curled around the edge of her pillow, gripping it tight.

She could feel her heart shattering, breaking piece by piece.

"Oh God…
 why?

Why did you give me this heart, this love,

If it only means pain?

Why did you make me this person,

If all I do is bring suffering?"

She closed her eyes.

Her breath was ragged, heavy, drowning in sorrow.

"I think I should take a strong decision.

I should leave them. Forever."

And in that moment, as silence swallowed her whole,
Sitara knew—

She was about to break her own heart.

Chapter 31
The House Where She Left Everything

The morning felt heavier than the night.

A silence too deafening, a void too consuming.

Aniket woke up with a strange feeling in his chest,
like something was slipping through his fingers,
like something precious was about to be lost.

He didn't bother with coffee, didn't check his phone—
his feet carried him straight to her room.
But the moment he pushed the door open, his breath
stopped.

The room wasn't just empty—
it was erased.
Not a single trace of her,
not a single forgotten belonging,
not even a crumpled piece of paper that might whisper her
last thoughts.
Nothing.

It was as if she had never been here.

As if she had never belonged.

His chest tightened; his hands trembled.

He took a step inside, then another.

"Sitara…?"

His voice barely made a sound, lost in the hollow emptiness.

But he knew.
She was gone.

And she hadn't even left him a goodbye.

Not that he was expecting one—
but he had hoped.

He had hoped she would at least fight with him before leaving.
That she would yell at him, blame him, throw things, cry—anything but this.

But no.

She had done what she always did.

She had disappeared.

And he was left with nothing but the unbearable ache of her absence.

The Search

Aniket, Chintu, and Saanvi searched everywhere.

Her resort.

The shooting sets.

Every place she had ever laughed, cried, or spent a quiet evening.

But Sitara was nowhere.

The city felt too big without her,
the roads too unfamiliar,
as if the air itself refused to hold her scent anymore.

Aniket gritted his teeth, frustration mixing with something darker fear.

"She wouldn't just vanish like this."

Saanvi's voice was calm, but her eyes betrayed her worry.

"Anni… this isn't just about Bittu.
This is something deeper.

She's always believed that love is a curse for her."
Aniket clenched his fists.

"She can believe whatever the hell she wants.
But she can't just run away from us.

Not this time.

Not from me."

Chintu exhaled sharply. "Where else do we look?"

A heavy silence settled between them.

And then, as if struck by lightning, Saanvi whispered—
"Her mother's house."

Aniket turned to her, heart hammering.

"Where is it?"
Saanvi looked away, her voice almost breaking.

"None of us know."
For the first time in years,

Aniket felt completely powerless.

She had gone back to the one place where no one could
find her.
The house where she had left everything behind.
And maybe…

This time, she didn't plan to come back.

Chapter 32
Hate

Half a day had passed, and there was no trace of her. The sinking feeling in Aniket's chest grew heavier with every passing second. He had searched everywhere, but Sitara was nowhere to be found. A dark thought crossed his mind, something he didn't want to believe, but it gnawed at him relentlessly.

Turning to Saanvi, he asked, "Do you know where her mom is buried?"

Saanvi's face fell. She hesitated, then nodded. "Yeah... I know."

Without wasting another moment, they rushed to the burial site. The place was quiet, untouched by time, except for a fresh mound of dirt. And there she was—Sitara.

She was sitting there, her arms wrapped around herself as if trying to hold herself together. Her eyes were bloodshot, swollen from crying, her face hollow with grief. The sight of her, so small and lost, made Aniket's heart clench. His breath caught in his throat when he noticed another small mound of dirt beside her mother's grave.
Bittu.
She had buried him there, right next to her mother.

Aniket's chest tightened. His steps quickened, and as soon as he reached her, words burst out of him before he could stop them.

"What the hell do you think you're doing?" His voice cracked with frustration, fear, and something deeper pain. "Running away from us? From me?"

Sitara didn't look up. She just stared at the ground, her fingers clutching a handful of dirt as if it were the last piece of her world she had left.

"I'm just saving you," she whispered.
Aniket let out a hollow laugh, one that held no humour. "Saving? That's a joke, right? Do you even know that I love you?"

She didn't answer. She didn't even flinch.

His voice softened, desperation slipping in. "Sitara… this isn't the way. This isn't how you deal with pain. Running away won't fix anything. You're just hurting yourself more."

She finally lifted her gaze, her eyes filled with something unreadable. "You don't understand, Anni. I'm not running. I'm letting go."

He shook his head, stepping closer. "No, you're not. You're pushing everyone away. That's not letting go— that's breaking yourself. And you don't have to do this alone."

"I'm not coming anywhere, Anni." Her voice was firm, but her hands trembled.

His jaw clenched. He exhaled sharply, trying to keep his own emotions in check. "Okay… just tell me where you're staying."

She stood up, brushing past him, her voice cold. "You guys should just leave. Just go. Leave me alone." She turned to face him, her eyes flashing with something close to anger. "I hate you. I hate all of you. You always leave."

Aniket froze.

He knew she didn't mean it. He knew she was hurting, that she was trying to push them away before they could leave her first. But hearing those words still cut deep.

His voice was barely above a whisper. "Sitara… just saying you hate us doesn't change the fact that you love us." He swallowed hard. "You do love us, right?"

She looked away.

"Then stop this," he pleaded. "Stop punishing yourself for things that aren't your fault. Just keep your thoughts calm and come back."
But she wasn't ready to listen.

Aniket sighed, running a hand through his hair. He knew pushing her too hard right now wouldn't work. She needed time.

So, he made a decision.

Turning to the others, he said, "Go home."

"What?" Saanvi looked at him in disbelief.
"Just go," he repeated, his eyes never leaving Sitara. "I'll stay."

Reluctantly, they left, casting worried glances behind them.

Aniket didn't speak again. He just sat down beside her, silent. He didn't try to force her to leave, didn't try to convince her. He simply stayed, letting her know that she wasn't alone.

Minutes passed. Hours. Sitara remained still, lost in her own storm. And Aniket sat through it all, waiting.

Eventually, when she finally stood up and started walking away, he followed. He didn't call her name. He didn't ask where she was going.
He just followed.

And when she reached the house, his heart ached. This was where she had been staying. Alone.
She turned to him, her expression unreadable. "Why are you still here?"

He met her gaze, his voice steady but filled with something raw. "Because I'm not leaving you, Sitara. No matter how hard you push me away, I'll still be here."

For the first time, her eyes flickered with something other than pain. Maybe surprise. Maybe relief. Maybe a tiny bit of hope.

And that was enough for him to stay.

Chapter 33
He wouldn't leave

Sitara woke up to the familiar scent of home—the slight dampness in the air, the soft creaking of the ceiling fan, and the comforting presence of her maid, whom she fondly called Aunty. The woman had been there for as long as she could remember, treating her more like a daughter than just an employer's child.

She stretched lazily, rubbing her eyes as she walked toward the balcony, hoping the early morning breeze would calm the storm in her mind. But the moment she stepped outside, all thoughts flew out of her head.
Her heart nearly stopped.

There was a car parked outside. And not just any car. His car.

Her first thought? Great. Aniket must have sent someone to spy on me.

Her second thought? Wait. What if…?

She stormed down the stairs, barefoot, the cold floor sending shivers up her spine. As she reached the car and peered through the window, her suspicion turned into pure, unfiltered shock.
It was him.
Aniket.

He was slouched in the driver's seat, his head resting awkwardly against the window, fast asleep. His hair was an absolute mess, his face unshaven, and there was a faint line of drool threatening to escape from the corner of his lips.

For a moment, Sitara just stood there, baffled.

Did he sleep in his car? Outside my house?

Then, her shock turned into frustration.

She banged on the window.
Hard.

Aniket jolted awake with a start, looking around in confusion before his eyes landed on her. A slow, lazy smile stretched across his face as he rolled down the window.

"Good morning, sunshine." His voice was hoarse from sleep.

"Anni, what the hell are you doing here?" she hissed.

He yawned, stretching like he was in his own bed. "Sleeping."

"In your car?"
"Well, yeah. It's my car, my wish." He smirked, "Just like you do whatever you want, I can too."

Her eyes narrowed. "Mr. Lawyer, this might be your car, but this is my place." She crossed her arms. "I swear, I will file a complaint against you and your nonsense."

Aniket sat up straight, pretending to look serious. "Okay."

Then, without a care in the world, he leaned back and closed his eyes again.

She stared at him, dumbfounded. "Did you just go back to sleep?!"

"Mhmm."

"Oh my God," she muttered under her breath, looking up at the sky like it held the patience she was desperately trying to summon.

She grabbed the car door handle and yanked it open. "Get out!"

Aniket groaned, cracking one eye open. "Sitara, it's too early for drama."

"Early? You slept in your car outside my house! If anyone sees you, do you know what they'll think?"

"That I'm an amazing, committed man who just wanted to be close to the love of his life?"

Sitara's jaw dropped. "Are you for real?"

Aniket grinned, sitting up properly. "Look, if you're that worried, let's make it simple. Just let me inside."

"Excuse me?"

He stretched again, looking at her like it was the most obvious solution in the world. "If I'm inside the house, no one will see me outside. Problem solved."

Her head was spinning. This man was impossible.

She pointed a finger at him. "You are unbelievable."
He winked. "And yet, here I am. Believable enough to be standing in front of you."

She groaned, throwing her hands up. "Fine! Do whatever you want. Sleep in your car, camp outside, turn into a statue for all I care."

With that, she stomped back inside.

Aniket chuckled, shaking his head as he leaned back in his seat. Challenge accepted, Sitara. Let's see how long you can ignore me.

Chapter 34
The Relentless guest

Three days.

For three whole days, Sitara had watched the same ridiculous routine unfold right outside her house.

Aniket would go to work in the morning, come back in the evening, park his car in front of her gate, and—like clockwork—spend the night sleeping in it.

At first, she had ignored him, hoping he would eventually get tired of his nonsense and leave. But no. Anikct was like a stubborn stain on her life, refusing to fade away.

On the third night, she found herself peeking out from her bedroom window, arms crossed, watching him with narrowed eyes. He was in his usual spot, slouched back in the driver's seat, his eyes closed as if he had all the time in the world.

Her frustration was building.

"What is he even trying to prove?" she muttered under her breath.

Just then, Aunty walked up beside her, carrying a steaming cup of tea. She followed Sitara's gaze and sighed. "Still there, huh?"

"Yes," Sitara groaned. "Like an uninvited guest who doesn't understand that the party is over."

Aunty sipped her tea, studying Aniket for a moment. "Is he your lover?"

Sitara nearly choked. "What?! No!"

Aunty raised an eyebrow. "Then what does he want?"

"I—" Sitara opened her mouth but had no answer. What did he want?

Aunty shook her head knowingly. "He must love you a lot."

Sitara scoffed. "Love? This is madness."

Aunty gave her a pointed look. "Madness is sleeping in a car for three days outside someone's house. Love is what makes a man choose to do something that crazy."

Sitara had no response to that.

Aunty placed a gentle hand on her shoulder. "Let him in. We have plenty of rooms in this house."

Sitara turned to her in disbelief. "You want me to invite him inside? Aunty, have you lost it?"

Aunty simply smiled and walked away, leaving Sitara fuming.

Downstairs, however, Aunty had already been plotting. Earlier that day, she had gone straight up to Aniket and knocked on his car window.

"Boy," she said, crossing her arms, "this is not how you win a woman's heart. Sleeping in a car won't make her suddenly fall in love with you."

Aniket grinned. "I'm just giving her time. She'll come around."

Aunty clicked her tongue. "And what if she doesn't?"

"She will."
Aunty sighed. "Listen, just sitting here isn't enough. If you really want to be close to her, why don't you just rent a room here? This house is huge, and I'm sure I can convince her to let you stay."

Aniket's face lit up instantly. "Aunty, I like the way you think."

So now, as Sitara stepped outside, ready to yell at him once again, Aniket met her with a casual, almost smug expression.

She narrowed her eyes. "What now?"

"I want to rent a room in your house."
Sitara blinked. "You what?"

Aniket pointed at the house. "A room. Inside. With a bed, four walls, maybe even a fan if you're feeling generous."

She looked back and forth between him and Aunty, suspicion filling her mind. "You two… talked about this, didn't you?"

Aunty innocently sipped her tea. Aniket just grinned.

They both shook their heads no.

Sitara's lips parted in sheer disbelief. "Oh my God. You did talk about this."

More innocent headshaking.

She groaned, rubbing her temples. "I cannot believe this is happening."

Aniket leaned against his car. "So, is that a, yes?"

Sitara glared at him. "You are the most annoying person I have ever met."

"Still waiting for my answer."

She stared at him, at his tired face, at the slight stubble on his jaw, at the way he was literally living in his car just because of her.

For the first time, it hit her.

This wasn't just about him being stubborn.

He really wasn't going anywhere.

With a long, exhausted sigh, she muttered, "Fine. You can rent a room."

Aniket pumped his fist in victory. "Yes!"

She shot him a glare. "On one condition."

He raised an eyebrow. "Which is?"

"You stay in your room and don't bother me."

He placed a hand over his heart, looking hurt. "When have I ever bothered you?"

Sitara groaned again and stomped back into the house. Aunty chuckled, patting Aniket on the shoulder.

"Well done, boy. Welcome home."

Chapter 35
The Uninvited Guest Moves In

Aniket was shifting into her house.

Sitara stood with her arms crossed, watching as Chintu and Saanvi cheerfully helped him unload his things from the car. Their faces were beaming with excitement, whispering to each other as if this was the start of some grand love story.

She glared at them.

They ignored her.

She decided then and there: If I ignore them completely, if I show no reaction, if I make it hurt every time they try to hope—maybe, just maybe, they'll stop dreaming. And eventually… maybe, Aniket will leave.

But… was she sure about that?

She didn't let her thoughts linger. Instead, she turned and walked back into the house, pretending like none of this mattered.

But then, it happened.

Amidst the shifting, Aniket walked up to her, holding something carefully in his hands. She turned, ready to roll her eyes at whatever nonsense he was about to say—
And then she saw it.

A small strawberry plant.

The same strawberry plant she had left behind in the apartment.

For a moment, she just stared at it.

"I thought you'd want this back," Aniket said, his voice softer than usual.

She swallowed, reaching out to take it. Her fingers brushed against his as she did.

And then, before she could stop it, a smile flickered across her lips. Just for a second. Just a fraction of a second. But Aniket saw it.

He grinned. "You smiled."

Sitara's face hardened instantly. "No, I didn't."

"Yes, you did."

"I did not."
"Chintu, did you see her smile?"
Chintu, who had been stuffing a bag of chips into his mouth, nodded enthusiastically. "Oh, she totally did."

Sitara shot Chintu a death glare. "Chintu, do you value your life?"
Chintu immediately shook his head. "Nope, but I do value entertainment."

Saanvi smirked. "At this rate, we should start preparing for their wedding."

Sitara exhaled sharply and turned to Aniket. "Where are your books? Just hurry up and move in so we can all get this over with."

Aniket, amused, picked up one of his law books.

"There's an empty room in the house," Sitara said casually. "You can use it as your office."

That made Aniket freeze. He blinked at her, almost in disbelief.

Because just a while ago—back when they were still in the apartment—they had fought over the spare third room like two kids fighting over the last slice of pizza.

And now… she was giving him a whole room.
She was acting indifferent, pretending like it meant nothing. But Aniket saw through her. She might have been playing this cold, distant game, but he knew.

Deep down, she still cared.

Deep down, she still loved them as much as they loved her.

And no matter how hard she tried; she couldn't hide that.

Chintu, watching the moment unfold, decided to ruin it in true Chintu fashion.

"By the way, Anni," he said, smirking, "if you need any romantic background music while shifting, I have a playlist called Hopelessly in Love with Sitara—"

"GET OUT!" Sitara yelled.

Chintu ran for his life.

Saanvi laughed.

Aniket smiled.

This was going to be fun.

Chapter 36
The Weight of Unspoken Truths

Sitara sat in the garden, her fingers tracing patterns in the damp earth, lost in thought. The air smelled of rain and jasmine, but her mind was clouded by something far heavier—something she couldn't name, yet it sat on her chest like an unbearable weight.

Aniket was changing. He was always the kind of man who lived by structure, discipline, and a life meticulously planned. Yet, here he was, doing things that didn't make sense, breaking his own rules—for her. And she didn't know how to accept it.

She couldn't even understand it.

It unsettled her, watching him get close to Aunty, seeing Aunty support him so openly. Aunty had always been on her side, but now she called her Sitara Putta in the same breath as she defended Aniket.

Sitara sighed, rubbing her temples. Maybe I just don't know how to be loved this way.

The soft creak of the garden gate made her lift her head. Aunty walked toward her, her gentle, knowing eyes filled with something unspoken.

"Sitara Putta," Aunty said, her voice quiet yet firm. "Do you know when your father got cancer?"
Sitara's brows furrowed. "When I was in sixth grade."

Aunty shook her head. "No, child. That was when you found out. But he had cancer before you were even born."

Sitara stilled.

"What?"

She barely heard her own voice. It felt distant, like it belonged to someone else.

Aunty sat beside her, taking her cold hands into warm ones. "Your father was sick while you were still in your mother's womb, Sitara. The doctors said he wouldn't make it. But he did. And do you know what he used to say to your mother?"

Sitara shook her head, unable to form words.

"He used to say that you were his luck. That you brought him back from the edge. That you gave him thirteen more years of life."

Sitara opened her mouth, then closed it. She had spent so long believing something else—something twisted, something cruel.
But I thought...

Aunty smiled sadly. "Wrong thought, child."

The wind picked up, rustling the leaves, whispering around them.

Aunty continued, her voice softer now, like she was afraid to break something already fragile. "And there's something else you should know. The day your mother had her accident… do you remember what you told her before she left?"

Sitara felt her stomach drop.

A memory resurfaced; one she had buried deep. A younger version of herself, angry, impatient. Her mother leaving again. Always leaving. And she had snapped.

"Go. And don't come back."

She hadn't meant it.

But she had said it.

And her mother… hadn't come back.

Her throat tightened. "I—"

"I was there, Sitara," Aunty said gently. "I stayed with you that night. And the next. And the next. You kept saying it over and over again. That it was your fault. That you sent her away."

A tear slipped down Sitara's cheek. "Maybe it was," she whispered.

Aunty cupped her face, forcing Sitara to meet her eyes. "No, putta. That was never how it worked. That was her fate, not your curse."

Sitara squeezed her eyes shut, but the pain didn't go away.

Aunty wiped her tear away. "You need to stop carrying ghosts, child. Let them rest. You didn't bring death. You brought life. You gave your father thirteen more years. You gave your mother love. And now…"
Aunty hesitated before speaking again, softer than ever.

"…you've given Aniket something too. A reason to be reckless. A reason to lose control."

Sitara swallowed hard, her heart pounding.

"Give him a chance, putta. Stop running from what you think you ruin. If you truly believe that loving someone means they will leave…" Aunty paused, brushing Sitara's hair back like her mother once did. "…then know that you have already loved them. And nothing—nothing—can change that."

Sitara felt something crack inside her.

She had spent her life believing she was a shadow; a curse that darkened everything she touched. But maybe…

Maybe she had been light all along.

Chapter 37
29th of month

Every 29th of the month, Sitara arrived at her resort. It wasn't just a tradition—it was a duty. She made sure everything was running smoothly, that the staff was efficient, that every guest was getting the experience she envisioned when she is running this place which was built by her dad.

This resort was hers. Her blood, sweat, and dreams were woven into its very foundation.

So, when she pulled into the driveway and saw that familiar black car parked outside, her eye twitched.
No. Not again.

She stormed inside, heading straight for the front desk, her heels clicking against the marble floor like warning shots. The receptionist, poor thing, looked up and gulped.

"Ma'am—"

She didn't even let them finish. She snatched the guest register and flipped through it like a detective solving a crime.

And there it was.
Saanvi. Chintu. Aniket.
Her blood pressure spiked.

They checked in before me.

She slammed the register shut, inhaled sharply, and stalked toward the poolside.

And of course—of course—there they were.

Saanvi was lounging on a chair, oversized sunglasses on, sipping a fancy cocktail. Chintu was floating on a ridiculous flamingo-shaped inflatable, waving at the waiters like a celebrity. And Aniket? He was just there. Existing. Looking unfairly good while doing absolutely nothing.
She planted herself at the pool's edge, arms crossed. "Don't you guys have any other job but annoying me?"

Saanvi pushed her sunglasses down her nose. "Oh, but this is my job. Last time I vlogged about this resort, and people loved it. So, I thought—why not come back?"

Chintu grinned. "And I'm here because—"

Sitara shot him a glare. "I don't care why you're here."

Chintu gasped dramatically. "That's rude! I was going to say I came for moral support—"
"Lies."

"Okay, fine, I came for the food."
Sitara groaned. Then she turned to Aniket. "And you? What's your excuse?"

Aniket didn't even try to hide his smirk. "Do I need one?"

Her fists clenched. "You trespassed on my resort."

Aniket raised an eyebrow. "Trespassed? We booked rooms."

She exhaled sharply, trying to suppress the urge to throw them all out. Physically.

Then Aniket stood up.

And—

Oh no.

He stepped out of the pool, water gliding down his very unfairly sculpted body, droplets tracing the sharp lines of his muscles. His six-pack looked like it was carved by divine hands, his hair was wet and tousled, and the worst part. He knew exactly what he was doing.

Her brain froze.

Was she staring?
Of course, she was staring.

And of course, he noticed.

"You should stop staring at me," he said, running a hand through his wet hair.

She snapped back, shaking her head. "I—I wasn't staring."

Aniket tilted his head. "Then why are your cheeks pink?"

"I—"

"As far as I know," he continued smugly, "you're not wearing makeup."

Her jaw clenched so tight it could cut diamonds.

With a frustrated huff, she turned on her heel and stormed off.

Behind her, she heard Chintu cackling, "She ran away! Oh my God, this is the best day of my life!"

Saanvi giggled. "She totally blushed."

And Aniket?
He just smirked. "She'll be back."

Chapter 38
Letter

Sitara sat by the window of her resort, staring at the vast horizon where the sky kissed the sea. She had spent the night lost in her thoughts, trying to hide something that refused to be hidden.

Her heart.

Her blush.

Her feelings.

No matter how much she tried to run from them, they kept catching up to her in stolen glances, in his teasing smirks, in the way her heart raced when he was near.

The next morning, as she prepared to leave, she found herself hesitating.

She didn't want to leave.

And so, an excuse tumbled from her lips before she could stop herself.

"My car broke down."
Chintu, always the troublemaker, perked up. "Oh, let me check—"

Before he could ruin everything, Saanvi elbowed him, giving him a don't you dare glare.

"You can join us, Sitara."

Sitara pretended to hesitate, but her heart had already decided. "Fine."

She wanted to sit in the backseat, tucked away, hidden. But of course, fate had other plans.

Saanvi and Chintu exchanged a look before shoving her into the front seat—beside him.

Aniket smirked as she settled in, already flustered. "Comfortable?"

She turned her face toward the window. "Just drive."

And so, the journey home began.

Chintu cracked his ridiculous jokes, Saanvi exaggerated her stories, and Sitara… she laughed. For the first time in a long time, she let herself laugh—without restraint, without fear. She didn't try to hide her blush, didn't fight the smile on her lips.

Because in that moment, being with them felt like home.

And somewhere between the miles and the laughter, she decided.

Avoiding them wouldn't change anything.

If this was a curse, then so be it.

If it wasn't, then let it happen.

For the first time in years, she didn't want to be alone. She wanted to be surrounded by the people who loved her.

And so, that night, she wrote a letter.

A letter to him.

The Letter

To the man who made me run, only to make me stop,

I have spent my whole life avoiding things that scared me. Love, happiness, belonging. I thought if I pushed them away, I would never have to lose them. But then you came along, and suddenly, running didn't make sense anymore.

You are the mess in my perfectly organized life. The storm in my carefully built walls. The chaos I never wanted, but now… can't seem to live without.

So here I am, doing the one thing I never thought I would.

Saying yes.

Yes, Anni, I will marry you. But only on one condition.

I will never, ever say "I love you" to you.

Not once. Not ever.

Because those words are not enough.

Because if I say them, you might believe they are all I have to give you. But my love is more than just words. It is in the way I look at you when you are not watching. In the way I will stand beside you, through every storm, every silence. In the way I will choose you, every single day, without needing to say it.

So, if you accept me, accept my silence too.

And if you ever doubt my love, just listen—
Not to my words, but to my heartbeat when you're near.

Forever yours,
Sitara

At the bottom of the letter, she wrote:

"Some love is whispered, some love is loud,
Mine is the kind that never speaks aloud.
Not in words, not in sound,
But in the way I stay, never turning around."

She folded the letter with trembling fingers and slipped it into Aniket's room.

Then, she walked away.

She didn't know what his answer would be.

But for the first time in her life, she was ready—
For whatever was meant to happen.

Chapter 39
The Answer She Never Heard, But Felt

The night was a battlefield of thoughts.

Sitara tossed and turned, her mind restless, caught between hope and dread. Had he read the letter? If he had, where was the chaos, the teasing, the scene he would have surely made?

No. He hasn't seen it yet.

That had to be it.

And as exhaustion finally took over, she drifted into sleep—uneasy, uncertain.
Morning came too soon, and with it, him.

Aniket stood at her bedside; his voice smooth as silk. "Goodnight, darling. Did you sleep well?"

Sitara blinked up at him, confusion wrapping around her like a second skin.

This idiot. He hasn't read it. He always does this—messes with my mind, drives me insane.

If he had read it, he would have said something. Done something. But here he was, acting like everything was normal.

The weight of the night's anticipation turned into a desperate need—she had to get that letter back. Erase every trace. Take back the words that made her vulnerable before they could be used against her.

So when he left, she made her move.

Her heart pounded as she slipped into his room, her eyes scanning the space where she had left the letter.

But it wasn't there.

Panic clawed at her chest. She turned frantically, searching every corner, every surface—nothing.

Where is it?!

Her breath quickened, and just as she was about to rush out—

She froze.

There he was.

Leaning against the door, watching her with a gaze that sent shivers down her spine.
"What are you looking for, Sitara?" His voice was low, knowing.

He knows.

She swallowed. "Nothing."
But as she tried to leave, he moved.

A step forward.

A hand on the door.

A silent refusal to let her escape.

Her pulse hammered as she tried to slip past him, but before she could, his arms wrapped around her—tight, unyielding, warm.

A cage. A sanctuary.

A heartbeat against hers.

"What are you doing, Anni?"

His breath was against her ear, sending a tremor down her spine.

"You needed this, Tara."

She stilled.

"You're going to be my wife, Tara. I don't care if you never say, 'I love you.' I don't care if you hide your feelings in silence or bury them in excuses. It doesn't matter."

He pulled back just enough to look into her eyes, his gaze deep, unwavering.

"I don't need words. I just need you."

Sitara's throat tightened, emotions clawing at her chest. "But I—"

He placed a finger on her lips, silencing her.

"I got your letter. And my answer is simple."

His voice dropped to a whisper, one that carried through every part of her soul.

"Yes. I want to marry you."

And with that, he kissed her forehead—soft, lingering, sealing a promise unspoken yet understood.

Sitara closed her eyes, exhaling a breath she didn't know she was holding.
She never said the words.

But in that moment, she didn't need to.
Sitara stood frozen, her breath tangled with his, her heart waging a war she had no strength to fight.

Anni's words echoed through her—unshaken, unwavering.

"I got your letter. And my answer is simple. Yes, I want to marry you."

Her mind screamed a thousand protests. This wasn't how it was supposed to be. She was supposed to run, hide, stay behind the walls she had spent years building. But now, they were crumbling under the weight of his warmth, his certainty.

She clenched her fists against his chest. "Anni, this isn't—"

But he didn't let her finish.

"You said in your letter that whatever happens, you will never say I love you to me." His lips curved into the smallest smirk. "That's fine, Tara. You don't have to."

His fingers brushed her cheek, tilting her chin up, forcing her to meet his gaze.
"Because even if you never say it…" He leaned closer, his breath a whisper against her lips. "…I already know."

Her body betrayed her. The warmth of his touch, the way his voice softened when he called her Tara—it was too much.

She pushed him away—not forcefully, just enough to break the moment before she drowned in it.

"Ugh, you are insufferable," she muttered, turning away, gripping the doorknob. "And dramatic."

Anni chuckled behind her. "Says the girl who wrote a full-page love confession but still refuses to admit it."

She spun around, narrowing her eyes. "It was not a love confession! It was a logical proposal."

"Logical?" He folded his arms, amusement dancing in his eyes. "So, the part where you wrote, 'When you are near, the world fades, and my heart forgets how to beat like it should'—was that logic?"

Her face turned crimson. He memorized it?!

"Forget I ever wrote it!" she snapped.

"Oh no, sweetheart," he grinned, stepping forward. "That letter is framed in my mind forever."

She groaned, covering her face. "I should've never written it."
Anni gently pulled her hands away. "And yet, you did."

Silence stretched between them.

Sitara sighed, her voice quieter this time. "I don't know how to do this, Anni."

His expression softened. "Then don't."

She looked up, confused.

"Don't try to love me," he said simply. "Just let it happen."

Her heart skipped.

He wasn't asking for declarations. He wasn't demanding confessions. He was just… waiting.

For her.

For when she was ready.

And maybe, just maybe—she already was.

Chapter 40
Revealing to the World

Sitara never dreamt of a grand wedding—no lavish halls, no glittering chandeliers, no orchestrated perfection. She only wanted warmth, a place that held echoes of her childhood, whispers of her mother's laughter, and walls that had seen her joys and sorrows alike.

"I want to marry where I lived my whole life," she told Anni, her fingers tracing the old wooden railing of her childhood home. "Wearing my mother's saree, with only the people who truly know me."

Anni, standing beside her, listened without interruption, his gaze steady.

"And you?" she asked, turning to him. "How do you want to get married?"

A slow smirk played on his lips. "I don't have such a dream, Tara. Just a lawyer, a signature—nothing else."

She narrowed her eyes. "That's it? Just a legal contract?"

"If it binds me to you for life, that's enough," he murmured, stepping closer, his voice dipping into something deeper, something that made her pulse race.
"That's so... unromantic." She folded her arms, pretending to be annoyed.

Anni chuckled, tucking a loose strand of hair behind her ear. "Then, as you wish, Tara. If you want traditions, if you want every ritual, every sacred promise—I'll give you that."

Her breath hitched.

"Because whether it's in a temple or a courtroom, whether it's under a sky full of stars or just a dimly lit room…" His fingers brushed her cheek, tilting her face up toward him.

"…I will still be yours."

Tears pricked her eyes, not of sadness but of something too overwhelming, too vast to be contained.

Saanvi and Chintu took charge, turning the rushed wedding into something beautiful. A house adorned with jasmine and marigold, laughter echoing through every corner, the scent of old memories mingling with new beginnings.

And on the day of the wedding, as Sitara draped herself in her mother's saree, feeling the weight of nostalgia and destiny woven into the fabric, she realized—this was exactly how it was meant to be.

Not a grand affair. Not a spectacle.
Just her story. Just his promise.

And a love that neither needed to declare—because it had already been written in every moment they had shared.

Chapter 41
Vows Without Words

The house smelled of fresh jasmine and burning incense, the air thick with the essence of sandalwood and marigold. Sitara stood in front of the mirror, adjusting the folds of her mother's saree—a rich red, embroidered with golden threads that shimmered under the soft glow of the oil lamps. The weight of the past rested on her shoulders, yet, for the first time in a long time, she did not feel burdened.

Outside, laughter echoed. Saanvi was scolding Chintu for messing up the seating arrangements, and Chintu, in his usual dramatic flair, was pretending to be heartbroken. The warmth of familiarity filled the house, making it feel less like a wedding and more like a celebration of homecoming.

Sitara exhaled. Today, she was choosing something that once terrified her—belonging to someone.

"Ready?" Saanvi peeked into the room, her eyes lighting up as she took in Sitara's appearance.

Sitara turned, a soft smile playing on her lips. "I think so."

Saanvi's eyes shimmered with unshed tears. "You look just like your mother."

Sitara swallowed, nodding, her fingers brushing the delicate gold bangles on her wrist.
The wedding was not extravagant, but it was sacred.

A small mandap was set up in the courtyard, under the open sky. The scent of fresh flowers and burning ghee mixed with the evening breeze. Anni stood by the sacred fire, draped in a simple cream-colored kurta, his expression unreadable yet intense.

Sitara stepped forward, her heart hammering, but the moment their eyes met, everything settled.

He did not smile. He did not say a word.
But she could feel it—the silent vows in his gaze, the promises in his stillness.

As they sat by the fire, the priest chanted the sacred mantras, guiding them through the rituals. Anni tied the mangalasutra around her neck, his fingers lingering for a moment longer than necessary. The world blurred for Sitara. The flames crackled, the conch shell blew, but all she could hear was the unspoken promise between them.

"No love confessions. No dramatic declarations. Just this moment. Just us."

And when they stood for the saptapadi, taking seven steps together—one for trust, one for respect, one for companionship, one for laughter, one for strength, one for dreams, and one for eternity—Sitara realized something.

She had always feared love.

But in Anni's silence, in his unwavering presence, she had found something deeper.

She had found home.

Chapter 42
A Love That Needs No Words

The wedding was over, yet the essence of it still lingered in the air—the scent of roses and sandalwood, the warmth of the sacred fire, the echo of mantras blessing their union. Sitara sat on the bed in her childhood room, draped in her mother's saree, the weight of the mangalasutra against her collarbone heavier than she had imagined.

She was married.

Not to a dream, not to a fairytale, but to a man who loved her in silence, who understood her fears, who never needed to hear I love you to know that she did.
The door creaked open.

Anni stepped inside, dressed in his white kurta, his sleeves rolled up, his hair slightly tousled—still the same, still calm, still unreadable. He looked at her, then at the flickering lamp beside her, as if trying to find the right words.

But Sitara knew by now—he never needed words.

"Are you tired?" he asked, his voice softer than the night breeze slipping through the window.

Sitara looked away, playing with the bangles on her wrist. "A little."
Silence stretched between them, but it was not heavy. It was the kind of silence that spoke in heartbeats, in stolen glances, in breaths held and released.

Anni took a step closer. "You haven't eaten anything."

Sitara frowned. "I wasn't hungry."

He sighed, walking toward the small table where a plate of food lay untouched. "You always do this. Pretend you're fine when you're not."

She watched as he picked up a spoon, scooped a bit of rice, and held it out to her. "Eat, Tara."

She hesitated. Not because she didn't want to eat, but because something in that moment felt too intimate, too raw.

Yet, she leaned forward, letting him feed her.

And just like that, she knew—this was love. Not in grand declarations, not in poetic confessions, but in the quiet care, in the way he noticed even the smallest things about her.

She swallowed, looking at him. "Anni..."
He raised an eyebrow.

Sitara took a deep breath. "I can't say it."

He smiled, a rare, genuine smile that reached his eyes. "You don't have to."

And in that silence, in that shared warmth, in the flickering glow of the lamp, Sitara realized—

She had married a man who understood her better than she understood herself.

Chapter 43
A Love That Fought and Flourished

Marriage didn't change them.

Sitara was still Sitara—stubborn, fiery, and full of contradictions. Anni was still Anni—calm, teasing, and annoyingly right most of the time. They loved each other, but that never meant they stopped fighting.

"You're taking the left side," Anni declared, throwing a pillow on the bed.

Sitara crossed her arms. "I've always slept on the right side!"

"Well, now you won't."
"And why is that?"

Anni smirked. "Because I said so."

Sitara rolled her eyes. "Wow, what a logical explanation, Mr. Know-It-All."

He grinned. "Exactly. Now, move."

Instead of moving, she flopped onto the right side with a triumphant smirk. Anni sighed, pinching the bridge of his nose. "Fine, but if you wake up on the floor, don't blame me."

The next morning, she did wake up—half off the bed, tangled in the blanket, her head resting on Anni's chest.

"See? Told you," he murmured, still half-asleep.

She groaned, shoving him away. "Ugh, shut up!"

It wasn't just the bed. They fought over who would shower first.

"You went first yesterday!" Sitara huffed, blocking the bathroom door.

Anni leaned against the wall, arms crossed. "Ladies first, isn't that what you say?"

"Exactly!"

"Then go ahead."

She narrowed her eyes. "Oh no, you're just trying to act generous so I can owe you one later!"

Anni chuckled. "Smart girl."

But before she could retort, he suddenly lifted her up, carried her inside, and placed her in front of the shower. "There. Now you're first."

She gaped at him. "You're impossible!"

"And you love me for it," he winked, shutting the door behind him.

Cooking was another war.

"You burnt the roti!" Sitara accused, staring at the charred piece of bread.

Anni shrugged. "It's just a little crispy."

"A little? It looks like a rock!"

He took a bite, chewed for a second, and then quickly grabbed water. "Okay, maybe a big rock."

Sitara laughed, shoving him playfully. "Let me do it."

"No way! It's my turn today."

"Fine, but if you burn the next one, I'm taking over."

Anni smirked. "Deal."

Two minutes later, another roti turned black.

Sitara raised an eyebrow.

Anni sighed, handing her the rolling pin. "Fine, you win."

They fought, they argued, they teased.

But at the end of the day, when they collapsed on the bed, exhausted from all the bickering, Anni would pull her close.
And Sitara, without even realizing, would rest her head on his chest.

No apologies were needed. No "I love you" was spoken.

Because love was in the fights, in the laughter, in the ridiculous competitions.

Love was in the way they stayed the same—yet couldn't imagine life without each other.

Chapter 44
A Name Woven in Love

The night was quiet, the soft hum of the ceiling fan filling the space between them. Sitara lay on her back, staring at the ceiling, while Anni rested on his side, watching her with a playful glint in his eyes.

"Hey, Tara," he murmured, his fingers tracing circles on the back of her hand.

"Hmm?"

"What would we name our child?"

Sitara turned her head slightly, a smile teasing her lips. "Tarini."

Anni blinked, caught off guard. "Tarini?"

She nodded, watching his expression closely. "Yes, Tarini."
His brows furrowed for a moment before realization dawned on him. "Wait... Tara and Anni—Tarini?"

A soft chuckle escaped her lips. "Exactly."

Anni grinned, clearly impressed. "That's so thoughtful."
She rolled her eyes. "Took you long enough to figure it out."

He reached over, tucking a strand of hair behind her ear. "You always surprise me, Tara."

For a moment, silence settled between them, warm and comfortable. Then, with a mischievous smirk, Anni broke it.

"Now that we've already discussed the name," he said, voice teasing, "when are we having a baby?"

Sitara's eyes widened, and she smacked his arm. "Anni!"

"What?" He feigned innocence. "I'm just eager!"

She groaned, turning away. "Go to sleep."

He leaned closer, resting his chin on her shoulder. "Come on, Tara. Just imagine—a little version of you, with your stubbornness and my charm."

She scoffed. "More like your laziness and my sarcasm."

Anni laughed, wrapping his arms around her waist, pulling her close. "No matter what, they'll be ours."

Sitara sighed, letting herself melt into his embrace. "Someday, Anni. But for now, let's just enjoy this—just you and me."
He pressed a kiss to her forehead. "Always, Tara. Always."

Chapter 45
The Beginning of a New Chapter

Days turned into months, and their life together was filled with the same playful fights, stolen kisses, and endless laughter. Sitara and Anni had settled into their chaotic yet beautiful rhythm—bickering over morning coffee, debating about who left the lights on, and competing over who could make the spiciest biryani.

But then, something changed.

Sitara had noticed the signs—her unusual exhaustion, the sudden aversion to her beloved coffee, and an odd craving for sweets. She brushed it off at first, convincing herself it was just stress, but deep down, she knew something was different.

Instead of telling Anni right away, she decided to surprise him.

One evening, after making sure Anni was out for his usual run, she set up a small corner in their living room. A tiny box sat on the coffee table, wrapped in blue and pink ribbons. Next to it, she placed a note that simply read:
For the most oblivious yet wonderful man in my life.

As she heard the door creak open, she quickly took her place on the couch, trying to act casual.

Anni walked in, wiping sweat off his face. "What's all this?" he asked, eyeing the box suspiciously.

"Open it," Sitara said, biting her lip to keep from smiling.

He narrowed his eyes but did as she said. Inside, nestled between soft tissue paper, was a tiny onesie that read, Player Three Loading… and beneath it, the positive pregnancy test.

Silence.

Sitara watched as his brows furrowed, his brain slowly processing what he was looking at. He lifted the onesie, then the test, then back at the onesie.

"Wait… is this…?" His voice trailed off as he finally looked at her, eyes wide with shock.

She grinned. "Yes, Anni, we're having a baby."

For the first time in his life, Anni was truly speechless. And then, as if his emotions finally caught up, he let out a loud whoop, scooped her up into his arms, and spun her around.

"TARA! We're going to be parents!"

She laughed, half crying, half overwhelmed. "Put me down, you fool!"

But he didn't. Instead, he held her tight, his forehead resting against hers. "I love you, Tara. More than anything."

She sighed, resting her hands on his chest. "I still won't say it back."

He smirked. "Doesn't matter. I already know."

And in that moment, in their small, messy, beautiful world, nothing else mattered. Their story was taking a new turn—one filled with lullabies, tiny hands, sleepless nights, and a love that would only grow stronger.

Chapter 46
The Sweetest Secret

Pregnancy brought a new kind of chaos into their lives, one that was both exhilarating and nerve-wracking. Sitara, who was always strong and independent, suddenly found herself craving the strangest things at odd hours.

"Anni, I want mangoes," she mumbled one night, half-asleep.

Anni groaned, checking the time. "Tara, it's 2 AM."

She turned to him with wide, innocent eyes. "So?"
He sighed dramatically but got out of bed, grabbed his keys, and disappeared into the night. When he returned an hour later, holding a bag of fresh mangoes, she grinned.

"You're the best, Anni."

He smirked. "Say that again?"

"Never mind, just give me the mangoes!"

Her moods swung faster than a pendulum—one moment, she was sobbing over a sad scene in a movie, the next, she was laughing uncontrollably at Chintu's terrible jokes. Anni, who had always prided himself on his
patience, was learning a new level of endurance.

One afternoon, she sat on their bed, staring at the mirror, her hands resting on her small but growing belly. "Anni, do you think I'll be a good mother?"

Anni, who had just walked in with a tray of fruit, set it down and sat beside her. "Tara, you are fierce, loving, and stubborn. Our child is going to have the best mother in the world."

She looked at him, her eyes misty. "And what about you? Are you ready to be a father?"

He took her hand and placed it over his heart. "Tara, I've been ready from the moment you told me. I don't know everything, but I know one thing for sure—our child will be the luckiest, just like I am, to have you."

She smiled, leaning into his embrace. For the first time, she wasn't scared of what lay ahead. Because she wasn't alone—she had Anni, and soon, they would have their little piece of forever.

Chapter 47
The Beginning of Forever

The days passed in a blur of anticipation and love. Sitara's baby bump grew, and with it, Anni's protectiveness. If she so much as tried to bend down, he was there, ready to pick up whatever she needed. If she sighed even slightly, he was already on his feet, asking, "What do you need, Tara?"

"You need to calm down," she laughed one day as he hovered over her, adjusting pillows around her while she tried to sit comfortably.
"Calm down? My wife is carrying a whole human inside her, Tara! What if you're uncomfortable? What if—"

She pulled his face closer, pressing a soft kiss to his forehead. "Anni, you're stressing more than I am."

But in truth, she loved the way he cared. He spoke to their baby every night, placing his hands on her belly and whispering stories as if their little one could already understand.

"You know, little one," he murmured one night, "your mother is the bravest person I know. You're going to have her strength and my patience… hopefully more of my patience."
Sitara playfully smacked his arm. "Excuse me, I'm very patient!"

Anni grinned. "Oh really? Should I remind you about the time you almost cried because you couldn't find your hair tie?"

"It was an emergency!"

He kissed her gently, his hand resting over her belly. "I love you, Tara. And I love you too, my little one."

Sitara felt a flutter—soft, like a butterfly's wings. Her breath hitched. "Anni! The baby just moved!"

His eyes widened, his hands still against her belly. "Do it again, little one!"

She giggled. "It's not a trick, Anni. They move when they want to."

But a second later, another flutter, stronger this time. Anni's face lit up with pure joy.

"That's my child!" he whispered in awe.

In that moment, with his hands on her, their child moving inside her, Sitara knew—this was happiness. This was love. And soon, their family would be complete.

Chapter 48
The End, The Beginning

Pain. It was searing, blinding, consuming every inch of Sitara's body. She gritted her teeth, fingers clutching the hospital bed as another contraction tore through her. Anni was beside her, holding her hand, though she wasn't sure if she was gripping his hand for support or punishing him for what she was going through.

"It's okay, Tara," he whispered, brushing damp strands of hair from her forehead. "Just a little more, love."

She shot him a glare between ragged breaths. "You try pushing a whole human out of your body and then say, 'just a little more!'"

Chintu and Saanvi were pacing outside, unable to sit still, excitement and anxiety dancing in their eyes. The doctor had told them it would take time, but every passing second felt like an eternity.

Inside, Anni's heart pounded against his ribs. The room smelled like antiseptic and something else—something sharp, metallic. His vision blurred as exhaustion and worry tangled together in his mind.

And then—
A sound.
A small, beautiful cry.

The moment it reached his ears, his body froze. The weight of reality crashed over him like a tidal wave.

His daughter was here.

He was a father.

The nurse handed him the tiny bundle wrapped in soft white cloth, her face pink, her tiny fingers curling into a delicate fist. His throat tightened as he looked down at her, the world narrowing to just this moment, just this child.
"Tarini," he whispered, his voice breaking. "My Tarini."

But then his heart clenched.

"Sitara?" His voice wavered. His hands trembled as he turned to the doctor, panic clawing up his throat. "My wife—is she okay?"

The silence that followed was deafening.

The doctor's face fell slightly, her voice cautious, heavy. "We did everything we could. She fought so hard, but… she didn't make it. I'm so sorry."

The world tilted. The ground beneath him cracked open, threatening to swallow him whole. No. No, this couldn't be happening.
Sitara. His Sitara.

He stumbled into the room, still clutching Tarini, his breaths coming in ragged gasps. There she was, lying still, too still. Her face was peaceful, as if she had merely fallen asleep, but the warmth, the fire that had always burned in her—was gone.

"Tara..." His voice shattered as he collapsed beside her bed, pressing his forehead against her cold hand. "Please, wake up. You haven't even seen her. You haven't seen how beautiful she is. You fought so much, Tara, please— fight one more time. Come back."

But she didn't.

She couldn't.

Fate had stolen her from him, just as she had always feared. Sitara had always believed she was cursed, that whoever she loved would be taken from her. But in the end, it wasn't her who lost love—it was the world that lost her.

She was loved by so many—by Anni, by Chintu, by Saanvi. And by a daughter she would never get to hold.

Outside, Chintu and Saanvi waited, their smiles faltering when they saw Anni emerge, his face hollow, his hands shaking. No words were needed. They knew.
Chintu sank into a chair, burying his face in his hands. Saanvi choked back a sob, clutching her chest as if it would stop her heart from breaking.

Anni looked down at the tiny life in his arms, his voice breaking as he whispered, "She would have loved you more than anything."

The weight of her absence crushed him, but as Tarini whimpered, her small fingers curling around his, he knew he had to keep going. For her. For Sitara.
Because love never truly ends.

And even in death, Sitara would live on—in memories, in laughter, in the heartbeat of their daughter.

A love that fate could never erase.

Half and Half
Half a smile, half a tear,
Half a hope that disappeared.
Half a road we swore we'd take,
Half a dream left wide awake.

Half a promise, half a past,
Half a love that couldn't last.
Half a touch that turned to dust,
Half a bond lost to mistrust.

Half the vows, half the fight,
Half the darkness stole the light.
Half the words we left unspoken,
Half a heart forever broken.

Half a name carved into stone,
Half a soul now walks alone.
Half a fate that slipped away,
Half alive yet gone to stay.

And in the end, not half but none,
Not just loss, but all undone.
For love once burned, then turned to ash
A story told; a life once had.

ACKNOWLEDGMENTS

This is my first-ever published book, and I am filled with gratitude.

I would like to thank everyone who bought this book and supported me. A special thanks to my friend, who read it with so much patience and shared valuable feedback and encouragement along the way.

I am also especially grateful to Ankit, my cover page designer, who understood my ideas perfectly and brought them to life without a single complaint.

Thank you all for believing in me and being part of my very first journey as a writer.

Sincerely,

Sowmyashree S Talawar